My Kingdom

& other poems, short stories,
& short plays for stage & screen

The fiction of Quent Cordair
resides at ~

"As It Should Be"

quentcordair.com

Cover Art

Molly's Swing
An original oil on canvas painting by Quent Cordair.
© 2002 Quent Cordair. All rights reserved.
Limited-edition, signed-and-numbered giclee prints of *Molly's Swing*
and other Cordair paintings are available at ~

Quent Cordair Fine Art
1301 First St., Napa, CA, 94559
www.cordair.com • (707) 255-2242

My Kingdom

& other poems, short stories,
& short plays for stage & screen

Quent Cordair

Cordair Inc.
Napa MMXIX

A portion of the content included in this collection
was first published on www.quentcordair.com
& elsewhere on social media
© 2012-2019, Quent Cordair. All rights reserved.

"At Home with Heather James"
© 2009, Quent Cordair. All rights reserved.

"The Match"
© 2013, Quent Cordair. All rights reserved.

"Mujahid"
© 2014, Quent Cordair. All rights reserved.

"Silver Angel"
© 2014, Quent Cordair. All rights reserved.

"An Uncomfortable Silence"
© 2017, Quent Cordair. All rights reserved.
First performed July 7, 2018
2018 Cordair Arts & Wine Weekend, Napa, CA

Selections from *Idolatry*
Part I: *Genesis* © 2014, Quent Cordair. All rights reserved.
Part II: *A New Eden* © 2016, Quent Cordair. All rights reserved.

Previously published content may have been
lightly revised and edited for this edition.

©2019, Quent Cordair. All rights reserved.

ISBN-13: 978-0-578-51979-1
ISBN-10: 0-578-51979-8

Cordair Inc.
1301 First St., Napa, CA 94559
(707) 255-2242   www.cordair.com

*To my wife and best friend,
Linda,
who makes it possible.*

Contents

Preface ii

Poems

A Call to Stand 5
A Love Unloved 6
A Man 7
A Million Steps 8
Again the Angels 9
All Infidels Should Die 10
And Again the Angels 11
At Last 12
Beacon in the Night 13
Better to Love 14
Between Venus and Mars 15
Black and White 16
Castle Walls 17
Character 18
Confetti 20
Eclipsed 21
He Completes Me 22
I Speak Cat 23

Ice or Fire	24
If Only I Could Gift You Strength	25
Into the Night	26
Manchester	27
Mark the Lull	28
Mirror, Mirror	29
My Kingdom	30
Moon Shadows	32
Now and Then	33
Of a Hundred Prayers	34
Out of the Old	35
Parting's Sorrow Sweet	36
Pinks and Blues	37
Spirited Gods	38
Stand	39
Tangled Web	40
The Algorithm of Hope	41
The Independent Power	42
The Night Too Is an Artist	43
The Soul, Hungry and Restless	44
To Your You Being You	45
The Rock Lodge Addendum	46
Toast	47
Trim Thy Shield	48
Unbowed	49
You Say Kneel	50

Flash Fiction, Sketches, & Musings

A Proper Bourbon & Blues Bar 55
Ad Astra per Aspera 56
Alive 57
Another Dance 58
Butterscotch 59
Character Always Matters 60
For Me 61
Friends 62
Ice Cream Run 63
None More Wondrous or Impressive 64
Oh, But You Are 65
Opening Lines to a Story Yet Written 66
Panem et Circenses 67
Seventh Morning 68
Should We Pray 69
Steam 70
The Dark Deeds of Night 71
The Gravity Field 72
The Minutes 73
There Won't Be a Debate 74
Ultimately 75
Well and Fully 76

Short Stories

First Bite 81
Off Starboard 83
The Enemy of the Good 85
The Robin's Nest 88
The Match 91

Short Plays for Stage & Screen

An Uncomfortable Silence 123
Silver Angel 139
Mujahid 161
At Home with Heather James 189

Selections from *Idolatry*

The Fountain 231
The Dance 234
The Child 236

Author Q & A 239

Preface

For me, an artist's studio can be as fascinating a place to visit as the gallery or museum in which his finished work is displayed. Practice sketches, studies, exercises, works in progress, casual pieces created solely for the artist's own pleasure—while never intended for sale or public exposure—can be as wondrous and interesting as finished works that have earned the artist's signature. Over the years, I've been encouraged by fans to publish the writer's equivalent of such studio work—written sketches, descriptions, dialogues, style and period exercises, scene and character studies, musings, selections from works in progress.

This collection includes, in addition to an assortment of the above, a variety of shorter, finished works dating to before publication of the *Lunch Break* collection. Some of the poems and flash-fiction pieces will be familiar to readers as they were first published on my fiction blog and social-media platforms. The short play "An Uncomfortable Silence" was first performed in Napa this past summer at our Cordair Arts & Wine Weekend. One of the poems, "At Last," has gained notoriety in circles holding nationalist, anti-immigration views.

"The Match," one of my most popular stories to date, is on the theme of freedom of speech, in a time when this most precious and essential of our liberties is under assault, and increasingly, from multiple fronts. A few of the poems and musings, political in nature, were inspired by the latest presidential election season; they remain, unfortunately and perpetually, pertinent. "Eclipsed" was inspired by the glorious and unforgettable experience of viewing a full solar eclipse from the rooftop of a friend's home in Jackson, Wyoming. "Mujahid," the script for a short film, should it ever be made, would be my answer to those who choose, over the real values to be gained in this real world, the fantasy of imaginary rewards in an unreal hereafter—those who would commit mass-murder in hopes of reaping such rewards. "Silver Angel" was written for a friend who wanted to direct and produce a short film that could be shot on a single indoor set, with minimal actors. "At Home with Heather James" is an art-for-artists piece, recognizing and celebrating the essence and actuality of that to which one is responding, that to which one's soul is resonating, when experiencing a work of art that one loves. "A Call to Stand" is a most personal anthem, given the context of my having been brought up in a fundamentalist religion—born to stand, but raised to live on my knees.

Some of the stories and plays have been published previously, separately, as e-books—they're included here for the opportunity to make them available to readers in a print edition. Other offerings, some quite short, were never intended for publication, but in sifting through my files, folders, and notebooks, I find that I like them enough to want to share them for what they may be worth to readers of like mind and spirit.

To one and all, welcome again to my world, my way. Welcome to *My Kingdom*.

Thank you for reading.

May 24, 2018

My Kingdom

Poems

My Kingdom

MY KINGDOM

A Call to Stand

One man at war with Man's deprecation
Calls out to all men to seek no salvation,
To pick themselves up from self-immolation,
To turn from the gods of their own creation,
To stand up and face the day—
To reclaim their birthright to say—
I am that I am, before nothing I kneel;
I mastered the fire, invented the wheel;
I cast the bells true and set them to peal;
I am Man, for whom all else is clay—
I am Man. I make my own way.

A Love Unloved

A love unloved is but longing.
A song unsung, silence yet.
A hand unheld wants belonging.
A soul will seek till it's met.

My Kingdom

A Man

There is no defeat
But the final defeat;
Unconquered I am
While I live.
I will Be till I'm not;
Till I'm not I will Be
What I Will,
Unbroken,
A Man.

A Million Steps

Cool concrete beneath warm feet,
A minor pleasure, true,
But fortunes are of dollars made,
And dollars grow from pennies laid;
My cache, a priceless promenade,
A million steps with you.

Again the Angels

Again they called to heaven
When around them rose a hell;
Again the angels came from earth
In answer to the bell.
The hands that pulled them from the flood
Were human, each and all;
And yet they thanked the god they thought
Had made the rain to fall.

All Infidels Should Die

"All infidels should die!" they cried;
She agreed beneath her breath,
For to life the most unfaithful
Are the ones who worship death.

And Again the Angels

And again they called to heaven
When around them rose a hell;
Again the angels came from earth
In answer to the bell.
While flesh and blood fought smoke and flame
And kept the black line manned,
The thanks went to the god by whose
Own breath the fires were fanned.

At Last

It matters not which border crossed,
From desert dry or tempest tossed,
To waves of grain and freedom's sigh,
From womb's dark hold to first-light's cry—
You're here, you're here, at last.

It matters not what age you came,
Eight months or eighty years, the same,
What color skin your parents' face,
What faith from which they fled to grace—
You're here, you're here, at last.

Now eye to eye, measuring minds,
The hopeful search for justice finds
No honest man can blindly curse
One more like he in chorus and verse
Than different—yes, in essence we
Are species same, from nose to knee—
As equals born with equal right
To live and work and dream the night
Where best we may, and here you are,
Your place of birth be near or far,
Your life and loves as dear to you
As mine to me—and this is true:
As innocent till guilty proved,
Against you none are justly moved.

So come, let's toast to freedom's song,
And may someday you pass along—
It matters not which border crossed,
To nurse's hands or shoreline lost—
You're here, you're here, at last.

Beacon in the Night

*On seeing the lights of our art gallery,
still on, of another late evening ~*

Beacon in the night,
Beaming bright and constant
For those souls in search of beauty
Light and clean,
A respite from the hurry—
Garden of delight,
Created, sculpted, painted
By Eves and Adams scattered,
Gathered here together
For those souls in search of beauty,
A respite from the hurry,
Beacon in the night,
Garden of delight.

Better to Love

Better to love than be loved,
If both cannot be—
Though, too, for we paired,
Spun in love's gravity,
While blessed through our days,
Bathed in worshipful shine,
Dearer yet my beloved
Than being loved divine.

Between Venus and Mars

Crickets below, dippers above,
Night rising cool around the foxglove,
Floor of warm stone, ceiling of stars,
Jewel on the ring between Venus and Mars.
You'll find my address between Venus and Mars.

Striding the plain, mountains surround,
Strove to find flight, broke the earthbound,
Made from this place, evolved and sublime,
Blessedly born and right for the time,
Mastering all but the passage of time.

Tick the count down until thunder and burn,
Children will fly, no thought of return,
While I remain, wave to their wave,
Watching them wing from the home of the brave.
I'll keep the lights lit on the home of the brave.

Black and White

From white the spectral fullness breaks,
From black the breaking dawn awakes,
And yet the fool denies the ends
Upon which all between depends.

My Kingdom

Castle Walls

Peace, peace, but not a moment to be found,
No closet or armoire is free from the sound,
For now your enemies live here in your head—
Sitting at your table—
Waiting in your bed—
And who is to blame for their being inside?
What use, castle walls,
When the gate's open wide?

Character

The shuffling line from dock to deck
Turns up the plank to ticket check.
Those early on the rails above
Wave wanly down to ones they love;
A long look down to ones they love.

Mark the ship, her lines and seams,
A welding of designer's dreams
And builder's craft—but is she true?
Or will she break against the blue?
How will she fare against the blue?

New captain there, high on the bridge;
A ship so large, his privilege.
It's whispered that he's wrecked a few,
Though smaller craft, that much is true;
Not one his fault, that much is true—

Or so it's sworn by this fresh crew
And owners old with lifeboats new.
All's well insured with fading ink,
They reassure with touch of drink;
The trembling calms with touch of drink.

The seas ahead are known to swell,
Lift up to heaven, drop to hell,
Loom overhead till pounding down
To crush the air until lungs drown,
With howling winds until lungs drown.

My Kingdom

Threatening isles with teething breaks,
A glancing scrape is all it takes
Across a careless bearing laid—
The reckless bet by all is paid;
The helmsman's due by all is paid.

The wise will eye both ship and man
To measure both with skeptic scan.
The sea cares not for sentiment
Or fervent prayers to heaven sent;
It swallows prayers to heaven sent.

In character of steel and mind,
In ship nor man a weakness find,
On oceans' floors, if truth be told,
There lies more faith and trust than gold,
There lies more hope than gold.

Confetti

The town had all been gathered
By the drums of the parade,
To cheer the clown's batoning,
Monkeys marching in charade,
A troupe of donkeys braying at
Ten leathered trunks a'swaying,
While on seven hobbling horses
Danced a nimble boardroom maid.

Coiffed tigers whining, sniping,
From within their pixeled cage,
A talking head on soapbox red
Preached equaling the wage.
On stilts the ringling master
Promised imminent disaster
Might await a tightrope walker
High above the center stage.

The big tent had been readied
And they lined up every one,
To pay their hours and heartbeats
For the thrill of passive fun.
At dawn the cotton candy sticks,
Confetti stuck to dirty bricks
Is all that's left but to forget
The good still left undone.

Eclipsed

Their dance was interrupted
As the handmaid slipped between,
With silent glide, as was her way,
Her creases pressed and clean—
"Pray suffer but a moment, ma'am,
Then I'll be on my way;
You'll have him back for seven years
Through each and every day."
With graceful curiosity
The wife let go his hand
And marveled as his aura's light
Around the maid did band.
Her blackness moved against his white,
The stars and planets awed,
Till wife in wondering twilight thought
Her wisdom might be flawed.
But promise made the maid did keep,
Her turn but for a spell;
A flash of brilliant wedding ring
Told Earth that all was well.

He Completes Me

"He completes me"
—said the Sea of the Moon.

The Moon, he did reply:

"As she flows to my push,
As she ebbs to my pull,
May we dance ever thus,
Till the dawn rises full.
While the day may me hide
While she sails her ships wide,
She'll yet move to my shift,
I'll yet draw to her drift,
Drawing closer and down,
Till Time forces relent—
And into her wet gown
I plunge shimmering,
    spent."

I Speak Cat

I speak Cat.
Granted, I hear Cat better than
    speak Cat ~
And don't even ask me to write Cat
Or to interpret some of those strange
    Siamese or Tonkinese dialects ~
But Common Cat?
I speak that.

Ice or Fire

Some say that Hell is made of fire,
Some say of ice.
From what I've seen the oceans sire
I think I'd choose the ice or fire
O'er sinking to the sailor's end,
In darkening depths come eye to eye
With demons vile come round to rend
A flailing feast o'er which they'll vie,
One bubbled cry ascending.

MY KINGDOM

If Only I Could Gift You Strength
(for Joshua)

If only I could gift you
    strength,
    endurance,
    perseverance,
While all I can gift you is the knowledge
That I, among others, so want you to have it,
To find it,
To keep finding it,
    somehow,
Whatever it is,
Whatever it takes,
    to live.
Live, please,
    whatever it takes.
Thank you.

Into the Night

And into the night
The writer goes to write,
Through the door between
This World and That,
Through the door which,
Upon his return before morn,
Has always been found to have remained,
At least so far,
    open. ~

My Kingdom

Manchester

Again comes the cry, again comes the mourn,
Clutched fingers in hair over flowers forlorn,
Candles all lit till the night wetly glows,
Coffins wrapped neatly in black satin bows.

Shadows beg mercy where mercy's unknown,
Prayers and peace offerings all fruitlessly sown,
The desperately hoping more love will suffice
For those taking no less than blood sacrifice.

There's left but one answer to those who love death,
Whose sword demands kneeling until the last breath,
Those blinded to reason, faith shrouding their eyes
Till torn from their skulls as their creed's final prize.

There's left but one choice, for those who love life,
In answer to those sworn to murder and strife:
When faith-deafened minds every argument shun,
When no word can turn what no logic has won,
When pleas have been met every time with a gun—
Swift granting of death is the deed sooner done.

Mark the Lull

Mark the lull on the battlefield
When Ideas have fought to a standstill—
In the silence hear the distant creaking wheels,
The shushed unsheathings,
The faint clicks of metallic intention filling
Cold, hollowed chambers—
For then come the guns.

My Kingdom

Mirror, Mirror

Mirror, mirror, on the wall,
Am I milking Life for all?
Am I tasting every rain?
Expending all for sweetest gain?
This day I'll hunt the rarest beast
For at day's end, my victory feast.

My Kingdom

My kingdom has no subjects,
No serfs, their backs to bear
The weight of lives of others;
None here are forced to share.

A kingdom filled with kings and queens,
Their castles great and small,
With princes blue, princesses true,
Good dogs to guard them all.

A kingdom built with brains and brawn,
Each year less brawn than brains;
We sow and reap, invent machines
That till the fertile plains.

We sail and dream, we wing the skies,
Beguile with arts refined;
We trade for riches far and near,
Hold forth in courts of mind.

We mine and dine, automatize
The tasks that bore to tears;
Our engineers, second to none,
Lean back and toast to cheers.

Our six policemen quite suffice;
We've seven hard Marines
And thirteen jets with bombs so smart
That no one intervenes.

My Kingdom

We welcome independent souls,
No honest man we shun—
Our markets thrive on goods well made,
On services well done.

Be immigrant or passing guest,
As equals all we greet;
New buyers all, new sellers some,
New friends and loves to meet.

My kingdom has no subjects,
No serfs, their backs to bear
The weight of lives of others—
Come join us if you dare.

Moon Shadows

*Inspired by Michael Wilkinson's sculpture
of the name.* ~

Moon shadow dance and moon shadow play,
Companion by night, dream of my day.
Bend to my bow and lie to my lean,
Moon shadow mine, till sunlight between.

Now and Then

The fractured image flickering over the millennia,
    broken and begrimed,
Healing for brief seconds, a few minutes,
    now and then—
The wholeness, the clean, bright view, coming
suddenly
    visible again
Through the curtaining Dark—
And the Age of Man
    yet lives.

Of a Hundred Prayers

Of a hundred prayers so desperate,
Sometimes one will turn out well,
And a hundred souls will pray again
For heaven over hell.

Out of the Old

Yet another year, she thought,
Sitting in her chair, she thought.
Still she might, she thought,
Still she would, she thought,
Till she did, she thought—
Her soul, willed and willing,
Rose and waltzed more lightly even
Than her body ever had,
Out of the old, into the new.

Parting's Sorrow Sweet

Though parting's sorrow sweet may be,
I'll have another course of thee—
The salted tears from silken lips,
The chalice raised on tilted hips,
Till lay me low in hunger's grave,
Contented still to still thee crave.

Pinks and Blues

In the day's death, pinks and blues,
Promises of morrows born,
Boys and girls and on and on,
Kisses and couplings,
Bedside supplings,
Until the day's death,
And the pinks and blues go on.

Spirited Gods

Spirited gods of body and mind,
Cleaving the earth and taking the find,
Arranging the atoms above in a bend,
Beneath which to dine, to dance, and attend
To desirable ends and needful things,
Burning the coal, inventing the wings
Upon which to soar like winged beasts do,
While raising fat herds for the savory stew,
Weaving silk threads, carving bone combs,
Harvesting timber for warm and dry homes,
Gathering the knowledge to hold in one hand,
On tablets of plastic and metal and sand,
Harnessing horses and nuclear parts;
Rocket plumes rise over rickety carts;
From building mud huts to high towers of glass,
From warring with spears to debating with class,
Climbing from caves to the moon and to Mars,
Masters of nature, eyeing the stars.

MY KINGDOM

Stand

Kings will rise and Kings will fall,
While Takers from the Makers haul,
Till Makers rising proud and tall
Refuse the Takers, Kings and all.

Tangled Web

What a tangled web they weave,
Yet cannot their own souls deceive,
In thickening threads a desperate dance,
Till struggling ends on Truth's sure lance.

The Algorithm of Hope

For Hope,
Take the sum of the Proven Past Good,
Minus Unfulfilled Expectation,
Over the denominator of Decided Deserving;
Multiply by the quotient of Depth of Desire
Plus density of Determination
Over length of Longing;
Subtract the Hours since
Supportive Evidence Experienced;
Add the variable of Unknown Hours to
Possible Fulfillment;
Multiply by the fraction of Patience Remaining;
Add the resultant value back to Patience Remaining.
Repeat calculation as necessary and able
Until the value of Hope falls to
Less than zero,
Or is lost
Between laughter and tears.

The Independent Power

For the sucker born each minute
There's a con born every hour,
But blessedly each day is born
The independent power
Who's neither host nor parasite,
Who's neither lord nor bower,
Who keeps his mind with sober art,
Before no king would cower;
He earns his take and pays his due—
A man, a sovereign tower.

The Night Too Is an Artist

The night too is an artist.
Having closed the curtain
Against the harsher lights
She brushes over the imperfect
And worn, reshaping the masses
In silhouette and shadow,
Softening the edges,
Leaving simplified forms
And the hope renewed
Of what might be improved
Come day.

The Soul, Hungry and Restless

The soul, hungry and restless,
Lives and moves ever ahead,
Traversing the desolate wastes,
Probing the uncharted wilderness
That lies between the heart
And heart's desire,
Ever hopeful of finding
A way.

To Your You Being You

To the best that's within you,
To your lift and your try,
To your will to see dawn,
To your laugh while you cry,

To your hope through the sorrow,
To your float over pain,
To your push through the dark,
To your dance in the rain,

To your rise from the ash,
To your straightening the bend,
To your fire to the lie,
To your go till the end,

To your cutting the knot,
To your swearing anew,
To your mind of your own,
To your you being you.

The Rock Lodge Addendum

(To Your You Being You)

To your lines and your curves,
To your lift and your fall,
To your crease and your wrinkle,
To your baring it all.

To your eye sparkling more,
When your trappings are shed,
To your glow and your smile,
From your toe to your head.

To your skin and your bones,
To your muscle and fat,
To each inch of you breathing,
To your you being that.

Toast

Our glasses filled with cheer,
We do raise this solemn toast;
Here's to all that we hold dear,
And to those we treasure most:
May you take all you can find;
May you keep all you can make;
May your heart follow your mind;
May you live for living's sake;
May you reap all that you're worth;
May your friends stay close and well;
May your heaven be on earth,
And your enemies in hell.

Trim Thy Shield

Trim thy shield in roses fair
Ere dawn's first battle cry;
Rest thy head in sweetened air,
When round thee vanquished lie.

Unbowed

With unbowed mind and unbent knee
Stands Man in full maturity,
With eyes to see and hands to bend
The Earth and Sky to serve his end.

You Say Kneel

You say kneel.
    I stand.
You say silence.
    I speak.
You say submit.
    I will not.
    I
        am
            free.

My Kingdom

Quent Cordair

Flash Fiction,

Sketches, & Musings

QUENT CORDAIR

A Proper Bourbon & Blues Bar

Napa needs a proper bourbon & blues bar. I need a Star Wars cantina kind of place, flush with locals and tourists, natives and aliens, with that hum of restless energy, the cast of characters coming and going, stories from here to there and everywhere, stories told and untold, histories embellished, half-told, masked, bared. With a relaxed atmosphere, generally, but always with the undercurrent, the potential for things to get serious, much more serious. And sometimes, just sometimes, maybe only once every year or two, the rising, palpable tension, the quieting and congealing to that blood-thick silence before the split-second move that will forever have the locals arguing over who shot first. Or who leaned in first, for the kiss.

Someone get on that, will you? The bourbon & blues bar in Napa, like a Stars Wars cantina? There's a corner table there, with a corner chair. My name isn't among those carved into the tabletop, but the chair is known to be mine.

This writer thanks you.

QUENT CORDAIR

Ad Astra per Aspera

There has never been a day when a man's world couldn't be infinitely better. There has never been a day when a man's world couldn't be immeasurably worse. There has never been a day on which better men didn't take the world as they found it and did the best they could to make it better with what they had, with what they found, with what they created.

MY KINGDOM

Alive

At our local bar, sitting next to two 70-somethings who've met here by happenstance. He was here when we came in, wears a medical bracelet. The seat next to him is the only seat available to her. And so she sits.

He's having a glass of wine. She orders a beer. It would be rude not to introduce themselves. They ask the questions, get to know each other. Only bits and pieces of the conversation can be heard, but the emotional undertones are timeless. He used to be in a band? What instrument? Saxophone? Her husband used to play! He taught her, but she was never very good. . . .

Heart rates rise as hopes rise. The cautious, cautious optimism. By the time he leaves, she's revealed where and when he might run into her again. When he walks out the door, his back is a little straighter, head a little higher. She takes her time, finishes her beer.

Another Dance

She had gone from expecting too much and forgiving too long to trusting too little and finding all wrong. She sat with her coffee, waiting for her next chance to walk through the door, determined to see him for what he was, to appreciate him for what he might be, and should they dance, she would dance lightly this time, with her feet on the ground.

My Kingdom

Butterscotch

We found ourselves standing next to each other. I was studying the prices of canned tuna. She was scanning the selection of instant-pudding mixes opposite. It was mid-afternoon, the aisle was otherwise empty. Try as she might, she could bend only so low to examine the items on the lower shelves, fearing, she admitted quietly, that her knees might fail to raise her. These things come with age, she conceded. We smiled it away. I turned to assist.

She was looking for butterscotch—that was the flavor she liked. If they didn't have butterscotch here, Target would have it. They always stocked butterscotch at Target. The prices were better at Target too, she said. Had I seen the price of cream cheese here? Over two dollars! I commiserated. Her daughter had found a recipe with her weight-watchers group in which canned pumpkin was added to the butterscotch mix—it was really quite good that way, and less fattening. That sounded good to me too. It would be surprising if they didn't carry butterscotch here, we agreed, as surely butterscotch was still one of the more popular flavors. Perhaps they had sold out. There were many newer flavors. We thought we found a few boxes of butterscotch towards the back of the bottom shelf, next to the coconut crème, but they were only a surplus of the vanilla. She would get butterscotch at Target. She thanked me, her eyes gleaming briefly, and we wished each other a good day. I continued along my way. She continued along hers.

Perhaps a half dozen times during our search for the butterscotch, she had reached out to touch my arm, letting her cold, delicate fingers, thinly gloved in fine wrinkles, linger on the warmth of my skin for an extended moment, for as long as politely possible. I hadn't pulled away.

She would find what she wanted later at Target. Here, she had found something of what she needed. I hadn't minded.

Character Always Matters

Character always matters. Always. The character of a man is who he is. Character is definition, self-made. It defines what a man will do, how he will do it, and what he will not do. Discount or dismiss the character of a man at your peril.

The predator preys at convenience. Awaiting opportunity, he employs camouflage, subterfuge, stealth, while studying and testing his targets' weaknesses, vulnerabilities. The weakness of many is simply their failure, their refusal or inability to identify the predator for what he is, their failure to take seriously the threat of what he has proven himself to be. . . . The mind, too, fights or takes flight. The danger is in the mind taking flight while the body, vulnerable, remains. . . . The predator lies low, slinks in, bush to bush through the grasses until he is within the herd. The danger is sensed—the subtle sounds, not quite right, the unusual lines shifting through the tall blades. The wary few raise alarm. The herd stops, raising their heads, scanning, listening. But the stalker has stopped too, holding, waiting—waiting until their guard is lowered again. The prey always lower their heads again, eventually, their hunger winning out over mindfulness.

Out of the thick silence, the dust boils and the strike is made. The screams of the dying long remain with those who escape—until it is forgotten again, forgotten that the character of a man always matters. Always.

For Me

I'm not so much against Islam as I am against religion.
I'm not so much against religion as I am against mysticism.
I'm not so much against mysticism as I am against faith.
I'm not so much against faith as I am for reason.
I'm not so much for reason as I am for life.
I'm not so much for life as I am for my life.
I am for my life.
I am for me.

Friends

"Evil's worst enemy," she said, "is the one from whom it has taken the most."

"Backed by the one with the most to lose," her new friend answered.

And with that they turned and, together, walked into the night.

Ice Cream Run

"A better part of living is not dying till you're dead." She had that indomitable look in her eye.
"Ice cream run?"
"Damn straight."

QUENT CORDAIR

None More Wondrous or Impressive

~ a musing on the theme of *Idolatry*.

Never has there been a god or goddess more wondrous or impressive than the wondrous and impressive beings after whom they were modeled. Man is quite incapable, thank goodness, of inventing an entity more remarkable or exalted than himself. The gods are nothing more, nothing less, than creations molded from Man's own characteristics, his own virtues and vices, his own qualities reconfigured and remodeled in effort to answer his own hopes, longings, fears, and uncertainties. The gods are, at best, reflections of Man's own essence, distillations of his own actuality, glorifications of his own potential. At the end of the creative day, however, though he may fervently wish or believe otherwise, no creation of Man can be Man's master. Though the creator may bow and worship the creation, the creation is not, and could never be, the creator's superior. The creation can be nothing more than the creator's servant, a means to his end. If the creator chooses to kneel before his creation, he is free to do so, but he cannot blame the creation for staring back at him in mute wonder.

Oh, But You Are

Oh, but you *are* an artist—you are the sculptor of your character, the painter of your style, the composer of your attitude, the architect of your future, the writer of the story of your life.

Quent Cordair

Opening Lines to a Story Yet Written

Man's most durable invention was the gods. He had always been fearful of trying to stand and walk on his own, and on the day when he finally let the crutches fall away, he was elated and devastated to learn that he had never needed them.

It wasn't a good day for the crutch-sellers.

Panem et Circenses

And came the hour for *panem et circenses*, for the promised bread and circuses, and the people's demands grew louder until they were given, not as much as they wanted or expected, but it was what they were given, and they ate the bread while laughing in the circus at the fear and pleading on the faces below, faces which had once been above. They laughed and chewed as pale flesh was ripped and bones broken, as the dark blood pooled across the circus floor, and when the cries below had gone silent, the people drifted home, sated and mollified for that day and the next, praising their new emperor and forgiving him much, until they began to grow hungry again, and the emperor was slow in providing, and another rose up among them, promising to provide *panem et circenses*, and faces below which had once been above.

Seventh Morning

"Every god was invented by an atheist, you know."

She had said it as casually as one might remind one's spouse that the post office was closed on Sundays. He lowered his newspaper. She turned from studying the cathedral across the plaza to signal the waiter for more coffee. Her hair was lighter in the morning sun, the highlights in her curls redder.

"Every god, you think?" he asked, his gaze coming to rest on her lips.

"Of course. Don't you think so?"

"I hadn't considered the possibility, actually."

"You will now."

She spooned raspberry jam onto her croissant and spread it liberally. Shifting her bare legs around to catch more of the sun happened to afford him a better view. A hint of her smile and a wink made him remember the night.

He went back to his reading but found himself obliged to ponder the invention of the gods, and by atheists, no less. He glanced at her again, over the paper's edge. She was absorbed, contently, in her croissant and coffee, soaking in the sun, watching the world go by.

He still wasn't sure what he'd gotten himself into, but he was sure he liked it.

Should We Pray

Having chosen their course, they stood staring at the path ahead, the shadows lengthening. Only the near horizon was visible.
    "Should we pray?" she offered.
    "Prayer changes only the clock."
    "And the clock changes anyway."
    She reached for his hand.
    "Let's go then."
    "Let's go."

Steam

The increasingly desperate fervency, the unshakable commitment and loyalty, the blind doubling down of souls answering the call of their chosen savior—there it is again, the pre-rational, primordial stew out of which so many religions were born. Where there is faith, there are those ready to follow; out of the churning, simmering pools of hopeful followers, leaders will rise. Muhammad, Jesus, Moses, Joseph Smith—how much was forgiven of them, how many sins and improprieties excused, overlooked, explained and polished away by those who told and sold their stories, all for the promise of salvation? The price of a savior—the ready offering of the mind, the sacrifice of the independent individual to the safety of the collective. All now to the temple in obedient lines, none minding the shackles tightening around their ankles, none suspecting that it is their own warm blood to be spilled, the steam rising and curling from the altar in the gray morning chill.

My Kingdom

The Dark Deeds of Night

The rain has come. The rain stopped before. It may stop again. It may not. Until the glooming wetness passes, it will weigh upon me like sackcloth as I wait here at the portal for the return of the bright and warming god. For what else can one do but show a constant and enduring faith? If a small rodent appears, I will sacrifice it so that the sun will reappear more quickly. The sun is pleased by offerings of dead rodents, a truth my ancestors have known and passed down through the ages. Until a worthy sacrifice appears, the emptiness in my soul may be assuaged now and again with communion from the human-priest's hand, morsels of sustaining manna for which I will cry out when he passes, shuffling by, he and his pale assurances of sunny morrows and an endless cycle of seasons. But what can he and his kind know of the sacrifices required of me and my kind to keep it all turning, of the taking of life necessary for life's return? Dutifully, quietly, I will do again what my kind have always done, knowing that the human-priests will raise their faces to the sun when the sun comes again, giving no thought or thanks to those willing to do the dark deeds of night that make the day possible. Yes, the sun will come again. Of this I will make sure. ~ Le Chat

Quent Cordair

The Gravity Field

She lay naked, face up, head to the north, feet to the south, arms outstretched, hands east and west, eyes full of stars. Beneath her back the lumped clods of dirt and broken carcasses of last season's grain, moist from the night's dew, served well enough for pillow and mattress, meshed with her hair, pressed against her bare skin. The cloudless sky offered no protection. She needed none. She took in the universe until she found her place again in the solar system, in the galaxy, feeling the earth and all its round wholeness—the mountains, the oceans, the molten core—not beneath her but behind, between her body and the sun. She had worked to shift her perception until she experienced the earth's sphere as it was, tilted, turning on its axis, her body held against its side by gravity alone, its surface curving down and away below her, leaving nothing beneath her feet but the great void. But she wouldn't fall. She was as attracted to the earth as it was to her, and she was dazzled by the distances the stars had come that night, each and every one, to kiss her body with light.

She lay there until the earth began to chill. When she rose, she brushed the straw and dirt out of her hair, off her body. She dressed and walked back to the limousine, shoes in hand. Her driver would follow the car's tracks back out to the road. She might not return for another year, or for three, but she would return, as she always did. Why else, but for this, would she have bought the field?

The Minutes

The passing minutes are of the irreplaceable things. Each comes into one hand and moves on from the other, while the sergeant keeps the line moving, always moving, permitting not one to come around and through the line again. Greet each minute with a ready spirit, a welcoming heart, and an eager mind—embrace each minute, dance with each, treasure each—some will bring you joy, some will bring you wonder, others will break your heart. Say farewell to the one minute as you turn to greet the next, and as the last in the line passes, you may find them all gathered there together, dancing in your ballroom.

When your departure is announced, turn at the top of the stairs and give your thanks, take your bow and your leave, and let their benediction sweep you out and away, into the cool and star-dusted night.

There Won't Be a Debate

There won't be a debate tonight. There won't be a debate, but there *will* be a carnival sideshow. Beyond the barker's tent flap, a garish display of two character-mangled freaks circling and clawing at each other, goaded on by a crowd thirsty for blood, gamblers flushed, calling out for their grotesquerie of choice to outmaneuver, dominate, and sink teeth into the throat of the other. There won't be a debate, but there will be a show. If I slip into the back, it won't be to watch the spectacle on stage, but to regard, to study for a passing moment, all who paid at the door with so many pieces of tarnished soul.

The night without will be cooler and clean, the tent's yellow glow and cries for flesh fading beyond the corner where the path turns to follow the river, where the moonlight rafts along beside, drifting toward the darkening wood.

Ultimately

"Ultimately, it's a love story," said he.
"Ultimately, aren't they all?" said she.

Quent Cordair

Well and Fully

Know that I've lived well and fully, that I've loved some of you more than you'll ever know, that I've liked others of you less than you think, and that my only regret will be not having lived long enough to see my enemies beat me to the grave.

My Kingdom

Quent Cordair

Short Stories

First Bite

"You shall have no other gods before me. You shall not worship the creations of man," said the creation of man—as told by the man who had created him.

And many who sat listening to the storyteller believed him. And the storyteller was pleasantly surprised.

His audience wanted to hear more. They demanded more. This worried the storyteller, as he had already told the three stories he had thought up the night before. To buy time, as was his custom, he feigned fatigue. When they persisted, he asked that they bring him food so that he would have the energy to continue. As the tent emptied, he pondered whether to craft a different story altogether, or to make up a sequel or a prequel to the story about the man who heard the thunderous voice on the mountain and the lightning that wrote commands on a rock. But the storyteller was fresh out of ideas.

The first to return to the tent was the young boy, one of the most gullible of his audience. The boy came humbly, bearing a basket of overripe fruit. As the storyteller picked through the offering, he leapt to his feet in fright—his hand had brushed a moving thing in the bottom of the basket. Perhaps the snake had been intending to enjoy the fruit for its own dinner—though the storyteller had only seen snakes eat other animals. He walloped the boy on the head for not being more careful, sending the boy crying from the tent.

Watching the snake's tail slither away beneath the tent's edge, the storyteller had found his inspiration. To spice up the tale, he would introduce some nudity. His prettiest young listener, always in the front row, would always blush and protest whenever he mentioned nudity or sex, but he noticed that she kept coming back. He would set his story in a garden of beautiful flowers and harmless animals. The girls always liked beautiful flowers and harmless animals. If he told his story well enough, she might be convinced to stay afterwards for a private story or two.

He smiled as the audience returned. The girl had brought him a leg of roasted pheasant. Finishing it in several bites, he sucked what was left off the bone and, nodding his approval, wiped the grease off his mouth with his finger. She looked pleased.

"This story is also true," he began, while they settled back into their places, having laid a small feast before him. "This is the Truth as the Truth has always been, the Truth as it has been passed down through a hundred generations of the wisest men, the Truth as it was passed down to me by the oldest and wisest priest of the tribe that held me captive before I escaped and crossed the desert."

The girl had leaned forward, eyes wide and trusting, ready to believe.

"In the beginning," he said, "God created the heavens and the earth." His hands moved through the air, shaping the story. "And the earth was formless and void, and darkness was over the face of the deep, and the Spirit of God was moving over the surface of the waters. . . ."

As he told the tale, he selected a piece of fruit from the basket and offered it to her, his fingers casually brushing hers as she took it. He watched her take the first bite, her white teeth piercing velvet skin, rupturing the flesh. The juice trickled from the corner of her mouth and down to collect in a drop beneath the curve of her chin. The drop glimmered and grew, flickering with the firelight's flames. When it was heavy and ripe, it fell, landing on the slope of her half-exposed breast, where it clung like a tear, rising and falling with her breathing. The flames were in her eyes, too, consuming his words, hungering for more.

Off Starboard

"Captain, I think you should come to the bridge, sir."

"What is it, Mably?"

"Here, look through the glass, sir. At three o'clock. A ship, sir."

"Where?"

"Closer in, sir."

"I still don't see it."

"Closer, sir."

"Oh—that. That's not a ship, Mably. That's a boat. A dugout canoe."

"What could they be doing all the way out here, sir? They're making straight for us. Do you think they need to be rescued?"

"If so, it won't be by us."

"But, why not, sir? Their little boat hardly looks seaworthy."

"They're attacking us."

"Are you serious, sir?"

"Am I laughing, Mably?"

"Well, yes, sir. A little bit, sir. But—how can they attack us, sir?"

"See those little blowguns? When they get closer, they'll try to hit us with poison darts."

"Poison darts, sir?"

"Don't fear, Mably. Unless they've found a new way to fire them, out of their arses or something, those darts won't make it halfway up to the gunwales."

"That's—a relief, sir."

"You're laughing, Mably. Am I funny, Mably?"

"Yes, sir. I mean, no, sir. Sorry, sir. May I ask how you know their, ahem, strategy, sir?"

"It's the same tribe that came out to us the last time we were by these islands. You can tell by their hair. You weren't with us then. They're the Moral Midgets of Microndria. Miserable little excuse of an island. But the inhabitants can be rather annoying if they get close enough that you have to hear them. Rather the opposite of Sirens."

"Can we use them for target practice, sir? The boys could use some fun."

"They're not worth wasting ball and powder on. We have real enemies out there we'll be meeting soon enough."

"So, what should we do, sir?"

"Nothing."

"Nothing?"

"Ignore them. They hate that."

"But—if they get too annoying, sir?"

"You see that storm front there, to the east?"

"Ah, yes, sir. I apologize for not spotting it earlier."

"Distracted by the wee ones, weren't you? Don't let it happen again."

"Aye aye, sir. Should we warn them about the storm, sir? Their craft doesn't look terribly seaworthy."

"Perhaps you should ask Mr. Darwin, Mably. Anyway, invite him up to the bridge. He'll want to see these."

"Aye aye, sir."

"I'm going below to play the cello. Have the first mate get us underway after Mr. Darwin gets his sketch or two and has a quick gander at them. And tell him, no specimens. The one we took aboard last time was complaining about the food within an hour. We had to throw him over."

"Aye aye, sir."

My Kingdom

The Enemy of the Good

Half the town, it seemed, was gathered at the front of the house, peering in, peeking over shoulders, querying, feral rumors slinking around the edges while, closer to the front, more respectable theories were being advanced in hopes of winning a laurel of knowledge for the price of a guess. But no one knew. Mr. Henkle was one of the most dependable, successful men in town, having led the seemingly perfect, enviable life, with the business, the home, the wife, the kids. Never a whisper of trouble. The news was unsettling, inexplicable. The world was no longer right. Everyone liked Mr. Henkle. He had always made sure of even that.

The sheriff emerged, a path opening for him through the crowd, but he answered no questions, offered no explanation, only studied the ground with furrowed brow as he made his way to his car. When the sound of the engine faded, the widow's sobbing could be heard leaking out from around the crossed-arm deputy standing guard at the door.

The gurney finally appeared, a rubber wheel fluttering aimlessly, supporting a landscape of draped white sheeting, peaked where the toes, chin and nose would be. There was no blood. The gurney's legs folded into the ambulance. The vehicle's doors were shut, one, two, more firmly and loudly than seemed necessary or appropriate. What remained of the man, the man who had been seen smiling his usual smile that very morning when he dropped off his dry cleaning, was driven slowly and forever away.

The coroner lingered inside, hoping to outlast the crowd, but the crowd waited, and waited, and he didn't want to be late for dinner. Black-coated, bespectacled, he came to the doorway, blinking at the low sun. Judging by the faces confronting him, he wouldn't be allowed to pass until he gave them something, something acceptable.

The deceased, he announced perfunctorily, had been found hanging in the study, suspended beneath the light fixture, the chair below him tipped and fallen. There was no note. No sign of foul play. That was all.

He stepped forward but the phalanx before him remained closed.

"What did he use?" Mrs. Beezitch asked. She lived only three doors down, and she needed to know. "A rope? A belt? A cord from the blinds—?"

"One of his silk ties?" Tom Greeley offered with a smirk, grunting when his wife ground a heel into his toe.

The coroner hesitated, but word would get out soon enough. They may as well hear it from him. "Well, that's the thing—" he said, his mouth pinching sideways—"Henkle was just suspended there in midair, by nothing we could see. Quite dead though, and for some time, head tilted, body and spirit broken right at the neck. Came down easily enough—whatever was holding him up wasn't much. I'll have to do a full autopsy, of course."

The crowd opened ranks, giving him wide passage, Mrs. O'Malley and Mrs. Sanchez crossing themselves when he passed, as if he were a priest come fresh from an exorcism.

Mr. Williams remarked to no one in particular: "You know, as good a man as Henkle was, I've always been under the impression that he was never really good enough for himself."

Mrs. Snow, who worked the breakfast and lunch shifts at the diner, was overheard remarking as she re-tied her apron, "For hanging yourself, an unrealistic standard is as good as a rope, I suppose. Just takes a bit longer. A shame, too. He was a good tipper."

"Sure, it might have been unreasonable expectations," Mr. Williams offered, not to be out-hypothesized. "You get a few of those twined together, you know, and they can trip up a caesar's chariot. Put a man right in the hospital or worse if he gets wrapped up in them wrong. It was unreasonable expectations that drove my Uncle Seamus to drink before tying him down to his chair for good one night. By the time we found him a couple of weeks later, it was too late—they had rooted all the way down into his heart."

"I'll put my twenty dollars on general perfectionism—" piped in Old Man Killebrew—"the perfect often being the enemy of the good, and Henkle being about as good as they come."

My Kingdom

That was as far as the speculation went, for the time being. The crowd dispersed, having generally agreed and conceded that they should wait for the results of the autopsy rather than spread rumors or risk starting a panic about anything that might be contagious. Yet the town was abuzz and unsettled for the remainder of the evening, culminating in an all-out barroom brawl at the Fatted Calf, the fracas having started as a polite-enough discussion as to what might qualify as an acceptable standard of perfection for fallible beings lacking omniscience and omnipotence, warming to an argument over perspectives on perfectibility as held by the Stoics and St. Augustine respectively, with the escalation to physical altercation being traceable to the glorious Molly McClennan's offer to demonstrate perfect form in cracking a chair over Tom Greeley's head should he fail to discontinue poking her in the shoulder every time he wanted to make a point. It was universally agreed upon afterwards, by those who had witnessed the incident, that Miss McClennan had given Mr. Greeley fair warning and that her form was indeed faultless.

The Robin's Nest

"You seek love," Amelie said, finally, emerging from her long silence. She was studying a ladybug that had lit on the hem of her skirt to wind its way purposefully, probingly along the line of silk stitches. She hadn't once glanced at Catherine since they'd stopped to sit on the garden bench. "Love is always worth finding, yes," she continued, "but it is trust I want. If only I might trust again. Trust is more precious than love, you know, more essential. Love depends on trust. Without trust, love is helpless. But *with* trust, love can soar. Oh, and how love can soar! Only let me find trust again."

The ladybug paused. It opened its wings once, twice. When it flew, Amelie's breath caught, her fingers opened reflexively, as though to catch and hold the tiny creature, but her hands remained firmly in her lap, her back straight, head erect as she followed its flight until it was lost in the buzzing haze. She pressed on, the words coming like an intoned rite over the laying of flowers on a fresh grave.

"When trust is broken, when trust is shattered, love can only stare in dumb wonder at the shards of its own reflection, rendered helpless again. When trust has crumbled into dust, to be carried off by the wind, love may persist, love may live on, but it can exist only as a bloodless shade, veiled in torn longing, shrouded in aching need, condemned to floating through the empty and echoing rooms, retracing the steps over and over, touching all the places again and again until the boards and posts are worn and polished smooth. When trust is gone, yes, love may live on, refusing to die, unable to depart, the unevictable tenant of a broken and empty heart."

Her eyes had remained dry, the tears all long ago cried.

Catherine shifted closer and slipped her arm through, taking Amelie's hand. "I'm sorry. I didn't know."

Amelie didn't pull away.

They sat just so for a while, silently, watching the bees work the crepe myrtle tree, flower by flower, the robin building her nest, twig by twig. When they spoke again, it was of things of much and little consequence, but nothing of love or trust. They talked together until the shadows grew long and the primroses were opening to the evening dew. As the rhythm of the crickets' song enveloped them, they fell into another long silence, a silence as natural and right as the first had been awkward and strained.

"We should be getting back," Catherine suggested, with little conviction and less desire. "We'll be missed." She felt a faint tightening in Amelie's fingers.

"If we must."

Still, neither of the young women rose, neither moved, neither wanting to risk breaking the spell, the spell with its suggestion of a possibility of something so unlikely that it might exist only in their imaginations, a possibility neither of them had anticipated, much less dared hope.

But in a moment that had passed unnoticed that afternoon, the prospect of a better, brighter existence in the world had been conceived. Somewhere within a warm and hidden fold of the makeshift womb of clasped palms and interlaced fingers, the seed of something wondrous and impossible had germinated and begun to take form. To many in their respective worlds, to most perhaps, what these two might dare hope to claim in that twilight hour would seem too meager a treasure, a coin too common, a half farthing one mightn't bother to stoop to retrieve had it fallen in a gutter. But for these two who had seen so much, two who had suffered more than any two should, two who had endured more than most could—two who had managed to survive in near complete isolation, on little more than sheer will, stripped of any and all hope—what they might possess in the moment, even if it proved only fleeting in the end and gone on the morrow, was enough.

In the last of the twilight, as they walked back to the manor, they were arm in arm, holding hands still, neither of them caring much at all, in truth, whether they had been missed. Consequences be damned. Before parting, they promised they would return on the afternoon next, to the bench at the end of the garden, to the sacred privacy of the primroses and crepe myrtle, to check on the robin.

It was only after they had parted, after Amelie had disappeared from view around the corner of the stables, that Catherine's legs folded beneath her. She sat in the middle of the path, one hand holding her body off the ground, the other clutched to her heart.

Though Amelie's tears had all long been cried, Catherine's first had yet to be shed. Her tears flowed now, the first and the rest.

She might have found a friend.

The Match

"Oh, Frank—this is gorgeous."

"I thought you might like it."

He pulled her chair out for her. It was a cozy, candlelit table for two in a private corner of the restaurant, with a view of the moonlit garden and the fire in the stone fireplace. The table linens were soft cream, the flatware was real silver, the china was real china. The champagne chilling tableside was from Elizabeth's favorite winery— their finest *blanc de blanc* too, not the label available in the stores. Surely this was a very special occasion. Could it be that he—? Was it possible that he might—? She didn't dare think it. Wouldn't dare hope it.

It didn't matter though, not really. Frank was more dashing than ever, with his fresh haircut, polished shoes and pressed suit, wearing the cologne she had given him for his birthday, the one that stirred her to her toes. Judging by the way he had been looking at her since pulling up to the house in the rented limousine, she knew she had made the right choice, with the little black dress and the pearls and the matching earrings. Simple, just like he liked it. "No distraction from the main attraction," as he liked to say. Sure, they were only freshwater pearls, but she knew he didn't care. She had found new shoes, too, for the occasion—black with laces double-crossing up the ankle and three small beads down the front to match the pearls. Tonight he was king, and she was, well, if not yet queen—but no matter—she was the happiest and most honored subject in the kingdom. His kingdom. All his . . .

As he returned the waiter's greeting, she continued gazing dreamily, unable to take her eyes off him as the waiter removed the foil from the champagne cork, unwound the wire and gently twisted the bottle. At the cork's pop, she started and suppressed a laugh. As the sweet, exquisitely small bubbles rose in her glass, she had to work to contain the thrill of delight and expectation rising with them. And

Frank—her dear Frank—was watching her face in the candlelight and smiling. When the waiter backed away, her eyes were moist.

He raised a toast.

"To us," he said.

"To us," she answered.

Already she couldn't wait for him to take her home.

How had she gotten so lucky? How could the second time around for her be so good when the first had been so bad? Single, divorced moms weren't supposed to attract the cream of the crop. Handsome, romantic, caring men weren't supposed to be looking for juggling-to-get-by working mothers with precocious three-year-olds—but there he was. There he was, sitting right across the table from her, going on six months with no sign of wavering. Her daughter loved him too, and he was as devoted to their happiness now, to both hers and her daughter's, as he had been since the first date. She'd have pinched her wrist if she weren't holding her champagne glass. She pinched her leg instead.

The waiter returned to inform them of the specials. Frank ordered appetizers.

"So, how was your day, darling?" he asked.

It wasn't until she was ten minutes into telling him about how her co-worker Janine was still making everyone in the department miserable, and how they were all trying to figure out what it might take to get rid of Janine, that she realized that Frank couldn't care less about Janine. Oh, he was nodding and mm-hmm'ing and asking just enough leading questions to keep her rambling on—but with his clever little quarter-smile, his attention would slip from her eyes to her lips, where it would dwell for a while before flitting down along her throat and further down to her plunging neckline and lower yet before rising quickly back to her eyes. He would ask another leading question to keep her going, his gaze hovering awhile before sliding down for another quick adventure—

"Frank!"

"Yes, love?"

"What did I just say?"

My Kingdom

"That your friend Wendy said that she overheard her friend Robin say that if Janine were hit by a bus tomorrow that Robin would be sad but not terribly unhappy."

"So, you were listening."

"To every delectable word, love."

She cast him a wry, wicked smile and glanced through the window to the shadows along the back of the restaurant's garden wall, wondering if there was an access door they could slip out through for just a minute or two. She wanted to kiss him hard and have him pull her body against his and not in a way that should be done publicly. A server brought the appetizer platter. She tried assuaging her hunger with a sliver of the seared foie gras drizzled with Bing cherry reduction on a crostino—which only made matters worse.

"Oh this is *good*...."

"This is just the beginning."

Just the beginning... *What did he mean by that? Just the beginning of dinner, or...?*

"Here, try one of these." He reached across the table with a morsel of baked Brie *en croute* atop a thin slice of crisp green apple.

Such a tease, but such an adorable tease. Glancing around to see if anyone was looking, she took his wrist, guided his hand to her mouth and took the bite directly from his fingers.

"Oh. My. God..." She didn't bother checking around to see if anyone was watching before sucking the juices off of one of his fingers teasingly, watching his eyes as she did so. Smiling, he pulled his hand back before she could get to a second finger. She sighed.

"I love you, Frank."

He only kept smiling enigmatically. What was going through that head of his? They ordered entrées—he, the porterhouse steak and grilled asparagus with hollandaise sauce; she, the Dungeness crab cioppino. The staff kept their glasses filled unobtrusively with deft sleight of hand. Two small salads arrived, the delicate greens plucked that very afternoon from the garden, arranged with an artist's care and composition, topped with accents of truffle shaved translucently thin.

"But enough about my day, Frank. Tell me about yours."

It was her turn to watch his face, the line of his jaw, the firm but supple lips, the high cheekbones, the gears of his mind spinning and engaging, turning, always solving the puzzles. And suddenly he was serious. She loved his serious.

"Well, we did make a break on the Johnson Hill case today."

"Oh good!"

"The murdered couple's debit card was used by someone in Portland. We've got video of the guy of the right height and build at an ATM, wearing a hoodie with the same logo as the witness here saw, and we're pretty sure we have enough of a license plate off the same vehicle from a security camera at the supermarket up the street."

"That's wonderful, Frank. You've worked so hard on that one."

"Well, it's not done yet. The car is likely stolen, if it turns out to be the same tag that was videoed in Redding, but we've alerted Portland police, and we're checking with the motels and campgrounds and the usual sources for the make and model. I'm nearly certain it's the same suspect from the home-invasion robberies in Vancouver and that he's working his way back up to Canada. We'll get him though."

"You always get your man."

"Oh, no, not always—but often enough."

They fell silent as their entrées arrived. Elizabeth's cioppino left her wordless, with its layer beneath layer of rich and subtle flavors— the wine, the garlic, the seafood, the broth, and some herb or spice that she couldn't quite identify. She insisted on sharing a bite with him. In turn, he put a slice of savory steak on the rim of her bowl.

Halfway through his portion, he paused and rested his utensils on his plate, finishing the bite he was chewing and swallowing— somewhat uncomfortably, she thought.

"Elizabeth," he cleared his throat, "there's something I need to ask you."

She stopped breathing. If this was *the* question, the timing was odd—but she didn't care. Her fingers were trembling as she left her spoon in her bowl. Clasping her hands in her lap, she waited, reminding herself to keep breathing. The gears of his mind were working again as he looked out to study the garden. Then he turned back and focused fully and resolutely upon her. He was serious again. Rather too serious, she thought.

"Yes, Frank?" She asked, blinking away her nerves.

"Elizabeth, do you remember how we met?"

"Oh, of course I do, Frank." She laughed, hoping she sounded casual and light. "You came knocking on my door—it will be six months Tuesday, next week."

"What do you remember about that first meeting?"

"You introduced yourself, so very professional in your manner—like you are now. You flashed your badge—" She lowered her voice, imitating his—"*Detective Frank Sullivan, ma'am. I apologize for interrupting you this evening, ma'am, but may I ask you a few questions?* And I insisted on inspecting your badge first."

It forced a chuckle out of him. "I had forgotten about that. It was the first indication I had of your intelligence and street-smarts."

"Street-smarts? Life-smarts maybe. I've managed to be smart enough to stay off of the streets for the most part."

"Yes, well, I think you have life-smarts in spades. Do you remember what I stated as the reason for my visit?"

"Of course, Frank. You said that you were assisting another jurisdiction on a case, the investigation of the death of a sheriff's deputy in Placer County."

"Yes, and—?"

She took a long, slow sip of her champagne.

"And—you said that my car had been videoed at about eleven o'clock on the night of the crime, heading west through the agricultural inspection station on Interstate 80, below Donner Pass."

"That was October 11th, the night the deputy disappeared in the snowstorm, but I never said anything about his death being a crime."

"Surely a crime was suspected, otherwise you wouldn't have come knocking on my door."

"It's my job, you know, to pursue all possible scenarios in a suspicious death."

"Perhaps we could define 'possible' and 'suspicious.'"

"Perhaps we could stay focused on the matter at hand. Do you remember what other pertinent information I shared with you that evening?"

She smiled sidelong and exhaled. "Yes, Frank. That my credit card had been used to purchase gas at about six-thirty the next morning, at a gas station only fifty miles further west of the inspection station, and that a vehicle appearing to be identical to mine was identifiable on the gas station's security camera at around that same time, and that there was no record that I had stayed in a hotel that night anywhere between those points."

"And?"

"Frank, is this really what you want to talk about tonight?"

"I'm sorry, but yes it is, Elizabeth."

"Well then . . ."

"What happened next?"

"Then Amalie came into the room. She got scared and started crying when I told her that you were a police officer. You spent the next twenty minutes or so trying to calm her and gain her trust, talking with her about cats and dogs, her friends and her dolls and her toys and her dollhouse. Finally, she let you pick her up so that you could help her feed her goldfish, Bradley."

"And what did I ask you next?"

"What you asked me next was not, I think, what you came to ask me."

"No—no, it wasn't."

She paused, took a roll from the breadbasket, and broke it in half.

"Would you pass the butter please, Frank?"

"Of course."

"Thank you, dear. What you asked me next was whether I was free for dinner the next evening."

"Yes, I did."

"And we lived happily ever after."

He finished what was left in his glass and glanced to the bottle, but it had been upended in the ice bucket.

"Would you care for more champagne?" he asked.

"Yes, love, but it's entirely up to you."

He signaled the waiter.

"But your cioppino is getting cold," he said. "Please—"

She ventured another bite. The cioppino had cooled, but it was still good, she thought.

Frank prodded at the remainder of his steak while waiting for the champagne. When it arrived, the label was shown for his inspection, the foil and wire removed. The pop of the cork caught Elizabeth by surprise again, but this time it sounded more like a gunshot and she didn't feel like laughing. The waiter filled their glasses and glided away.

Frank raised his glass solemnly.

"To the last six months," he said.

"To the *first* six months," she countered.

They touched glasses and drank while holding each other's gaze, neither looking away. She couldn't begin to read his thoughts, but he was having thoughts.

He glanced down at his plate again and seemed to gather resolve. Had his hand edged closer to his jacket pocket just then? Or was it toward—his shoulder holster? He always carried. It hadn't occurred to her, but of course he was probably armed, even tonight.

"I have another question," he stated, too calmly.

"Anything, Frank. Of course."

He cleared his throat. "You have a rather extensive and impressive collection of books in your apartment, Elizabeth."

Again, not what she was expecting, but okay—

"Thank you. I do love to read, you know."

"I've noticed that there are no religious books on your shelves."

He was using his official, police-detective voice again.

"You're so perceptive, Frank. It's one of the things I so thoroughly admire about you."

"We've never really talked about religion."

"I guess neither of us has had much to say on the subject."

"Given everything else on your bookshelves and your interests—the philosophy, the art, the history, the poetry—I would guess that you have some opinion on the subject."

When the waiter came by and lifted the bottle, she held her hand over her glass to indicate that she'd had enough. She studied Frank's face. He was nothing if not honest, completely dedicated to his work, scrupulous, a paragon of integrity, unflinchingly dedicated to justice.

No, of course he wasn't finished with his questioning. Of course he wasn't. She waited until the waiter was out of earshot.

"May I tell you a story, Frank?" she asked.

"I trust that the story would be relevant to the line of questioning."

"It may be. It concerns a collection of books."

"Your collection of books?"

"*A* collection of books. You'll have to judge whether the story answers your questions."

"You've answered every question I've asked so far."

"You may have more."

"I may."

"Well then—"

She retrieved the bottle from the ice bucket herself and poured from it. After a drink to wet her lips, she dabbed at the corners of her mouth with her napkin, hoping her lipstick was still okay. She took a breath and relaxed her shoulders.

"It's a story about a young woman, recently divorced. She had a three-year-old daughter whom she loved more than could ever be told. The girl's father—the bastard—had disappeared, leaving the mother to raise and support her daughter on her own. She didn't have any family dependable enough to look to for help, but after the initial panic, she found a second job and was managing—working two jobs while trying to be the best mother she could be to a daughter with whom she could never spend enough time. But she was managing."

"Sounds familiar so far."

"I must ask that you not interrupt now, Frank."

"As you wish."

"One of the jobs she took was as a personal assistant to a wealthy, eccentric elderly gentleman. She would do all sorts of odd errands for him: picking up his dry cleaning, cooking for him, finding someone to repair the gutters on his roof, taking him to the doctor, doing his bookkeeping. He was moody and irascible, usually ill, nearly always difficult to work with. He'd throw tantrums and teacups and implied that she was stupid when she couldn't read his mind or anticipate exactly what he wanted, the way he wanted it and when. No matter how well she did her work, it was never good enough by his standards. But the pay was just good enough to keep her gritting her teeth and going back again day after day. She was doing what she had to do."

"You're the first person I've known to use the word 'irascible' conversationally."

"I'm a reader, you know. But you agreed not to interrupt."

"I apologize."

"The eccentric elderly gentleman had an eccentric less-elderly son who lived alone up near Reno. The son died unexpectedly of heart failure, and it fell to the father's employee to deal with matters of the son's estate, including cataloguing all of the personal belongings, donating his clothes to a local charity, clearing out and dumping decades' worth of accumulated magazines and newspapers and such. Since the son's house was a three-hour drive from her apartment, she stayed at the house while she was working on it. The process of clearing it out took two weeks, and having no one who could look after her daughter for more than a day or two, she had to take her along with her.

"The house was a terrible mess. She organized the estate sale of the furnishings, the appliances and the saleable personal items. Many of the books and some of the magazines remained unsold after the sale. Of the books, there wasn't a large number, but the non-fiction volumes particularly were wide-ranging in subject and of mostly good quality. There was a fair amount of fiction as well, from hardcover classics to detective-fiction anthologies and even a few dozen romance paperbacks—the latter being an odd interest, she thought, for an aging bachelor, but having gone through his photos, she thought that he may have had a girlfriend once.

"With her employer's grudging permission, she was allowed to take as many of the books and magazines home with her as she could pack into her car. The sale had concluded the day before she was due to leave, and she had to spend all of that last morning and into the afternoon cleaning. Not having time to adequately sort through the books, she boxed and crated as many as she thought might possibly be of interest and loaded them into the car, intending to give them a more thorough sorting when she got home. The balance, along with most of the magazines, she left with a neighbor to drop at the local library as a donation. The only remaining item was a partial case of old wine she had found in the back of one of the closets. She made room for a half dozen or so bottles, tucking them between the boxes and bins in the car."

The waiter had reappeared, and though neither of them had finished their entrées, they let him take the plates. They declined the offer of dessert. Frank ordered coffee. Elizabeth waited for the waiter to leave.

"Please go on," Frank said. "You must know this woman well."

"I think you would like her."

Frank offered only a faint, inscrutable smile.

"The evening she set out for home, an early winter storm was blowing in. According to the forecast, the snow wasn't supposed to begin falling in the area until three or four in the morning, and under normal circumstances, she would have been able to clear the pass over the mountains by ten or eleven that evening easily. But the forecast was wrong, and her climb through the pass was slowed by the weight of the books. Her rear wheels would scrape the wheel wells whenever she hit a bump. The car wasn't much to begin with, an economy model that was old and always in need of repair. The engine was struggling up the inclines—"

"I really wish you'd trade it in."

"Frank, please."

He exhaled, resting his chin on his hand.

"The type of car isn't important anyway—even if it were identical to mine. And that's not to say that it is. Or that it isn't. . . .

"The authorities apparently had been caught off guard by the pace of the front as well—they hadn't yet set up the tire-chain stations on the lower grades before she was well on her way past them and up. She had never been comfortable crossing the pass at night, especially in winter, ever since as a child she had heard about the party of settlers that had been trying to cross there when the snows came early and they were stranded in the pass for the whole winter with hardly any food. The unspeakable things they had to resort to in order to survive—" She shook her head to clear her mind of it—"But there she was, with her three-year-old sleeping in the seat next to her, in an unreliable, overloaded car, trying to go over that very pass in the dark of night, with hardly any lights visible but her own and the snow falling thick and fast. The rising wind drove the flakes more and more horizontally until she could barely see in front of her headlights. Her pace gradually slowed to little better than a crawl.

"A few trucks and other vehicles passed her, but then there were fewer and fewer, and then none at all on her side of the highway or on the other, at least from what she could see, as little as she could see. After twenty minutes of seeing no one at all, she passed a semi-truck that had pulled to the side of the road, its emergency lights blinking, then two cars and an SUV that had slid off the road, one of them all the way down into the ditch. She would have stopped to see if anyone needed help, but her own car would skid at the slightest touch of the brakes, and she feared that if she stopped on the grade she might not be able to get enough traction to get going again. By the time she was truly and desperately wanting to pull over, she couldn't see well enough to tell where the side of the road was or if there was a shoulder at all, and the thought of stopping where a truck might come barreling down on her from behind was more frightening than trying to continue on.

"After what she guessed had been at least two hours of creeping along, straining to see through the swath of clear windshield that kept narrowing and closing in, caking with more and more ice and snow—she was running out of gas. She had no idea how far she had travelled when the needle on the fuel gauge was coming to rest on the 'E.' She was fairly certain she had gone over the summit. She felt as if she could have been descending for a while, but with no visual references, she thought she might be experiencing vertigo. Even if she had cleared the summit, she had no idea whether she had gone far enough to have reached an exit with a gas station, and when she did finally pass what looked to be an exit—there appeared to be a light somewhere above and to the right—she slowed the car to a stop. Unable to see through the rearview mirror because of the boxes and bins in the back seat, she put her hazard lights on, got out and cleared the snow from her exterior mirrors, then reversed her way carefully back up to the exit, fearing that at any moment she might see headlights bearing down on her."

Across the table, Frank was shaking his head.

For his benefit, she noted, "It might not have been any less risky for her to run out of gas out there on the freeway. At the very least she needed to find a safe, warm place to wait out the storm.

"From the top of the exit ramp, she turned onto the secondary road and passed what looked to be an antique shop, but it was closed and dark. The security light on the front of the building was what she had seen from the highway. A sign on the side of the road indicated that there might be fuel farther along at a campground, but the sign and any distance given was partially obscured by a layer of snow. Knowing that a campground wouldn't likely be open so late in the year, she opted to follow the two-lane a bit further anyway, hoping at least to find a residence with someone at home.

"There was a log cabin, but with no sign of life in it and no vehicles in the drive. There were no tire tracks on the road, and as the grade descended more steeply into the wooded hills, it became icier and darker and narrower until all she wanted was enough of a driveway or intersection in which to have enough room to turn around. At one point, she thought she might have seen a cluster of lights through the trees in the valley below, which kept her hopeful for a few more winding turns, but the lights never reappeared. It wasn't until three or four miles farther down that there was a hairpin turn which seemed just wide enough that it might accommodate a three-point turn—and it might have been, but as she was halfway into the maneuver her rear tires slipped off of the pavement and into the drainage ditch. She couldn't move forward or back. The more she tried, the more her wheels sank back and down into the snow and icy mud. Her daughter had slept through it all, so far.

"Are you listening, Frank?"

"Of course." His gaze had locked onto something in the garden. "I'm sure I know the road. And the turn."

"She kept a small flashlight in the glove compartment—"

My Kingdom

"That's smart, Elizabeth, but anyone traveling in the mountains without four-wheel drive really should be carrying snow chains or—"

"Frank."

He lifted his hands in surrender.

"Zipping her jacket and tying her scarf over her head, she got out of the car as quietly as she could, leaving it running with the heater and headlights on. Thankfully, the snow and wind had abated, though the temperature was still falling. With the point of a pen, she let some of the air out of the rear tires to improve traction. Back in the car, she alternated between forward and reverse, rocking the car to try to build momentum, but she still couldn't extricate herself. Back outside again, she gathered branches and twigs from around the area and wedged them beneath the tires. After several more tries and with more branches laid down, she finally gained enough purchase to roll free. Turning uphill, she made it a hundred yards or so back toward the highway before the engine sputtered and stopped. She was out of gas."

"They could have died out there," Frank said flatly, with only the slightest break in his voice to reveal that he might have cared.

"Well, you wouldn't have known them had they died out there, so it couldn't have mattered much to you—not that you do or do not know them presently."

The waiter returned with Frank's coffee and moved on.

"She turned off the car lights and the heater, and sat in the darkness, waiting, thinking. She hadn't brought heavy clothes or coats for either of them, just autumn-weight wear and lighter jackets. Her pant legs were already soaked from the work in the snow at the turn. There were two blankets in the car—her daughter's pink unicorn blanket and her own favorite quilt, in which her daughter was presently bundled. She knew that the heat in the car would dissipate quickly, and she wasn't at all confident that the shelter of the vehicle and their own body heat would be enough to keep them from freezing to death before someone might find them. She checked her phone. There was no signal.

"She sat and waited, and waited and thought, trying to remain calm. She turned off the headlights to save the battery, retrieved the unicorn blanket from the back seat and wrapped it around her shoulders. The only light remaining was from the glow of the radio, which was broadcasting only static—she had been so focused on survival that she hadn't noticed when the signal faded. She tried to find a station where she might catch a weather report, but the only station with an adequate signal was in Spanish and it was mostly music. She listened awhile, understanding little of what was being said or sung, but it was nice to know that there were people somewhere who were safe and singing and warm. It wasn't long before she turned off the radio as well—whatever the mariachis were pining about couldn't be nearly as tragic as they were making it sound, and saving the battery was paramount.

"Having slept soundly through the efforts to get the car out of the ditch, the noise of the car door being opened and shut, and the mariachi music—her daughter awakened at the complete silence. Tucking the quilt more snugly around the girl, she brushed the blond curls with her fingers until the little eyelids fluttered, drooped and closed again."

At the mention of the girl, Frank's demeanor softened noticeably. *He would make such a good father,* she thought. *Amalie was already so attached to him and he was so good and patient with her. Maybe there could be a second baby someday. Maybe even a third. . . .*

"She was exhausted but didn't dare sleep. With the snow covering the car, a vehicle or snowplow might come along and hit them if she failed to turn on her lights in time to make her presence known. On the other hand, she knew it was unlikely that a secondary road would be plowed before the storm was over. Worse, she remembered hearing that many roads in the higher elevations were left unplowed altogether, impassable through the entire winter once the snows began. She thought that most of the seasonal roads were gated with the coming of the snows. Had she passed through an unclosed gate? She couldn't recall. She might not have been able to see a gate had there been one.

"The temperature in the car was falling. She could attempt to carry her daughter all the way back up to the highway, but even if her strength held out, her flashlight batteries probably wouldn't, and if the wind rose and the snow began to fall heavily again during the trek, it could become difficult if not impossible to follow the road or to be able to return to the car, and they could be stranded in the elements without any shelter at all. Yet, if she waited until dawn, the snow's depth could be several feet by then, making the journey next to impossible, as it had for those poor settlers—"

The waiter had stopped by to warm Frank's coffee. Watching the steam rise from his cup, Elizabeth requested one of her own. There were still two other couples seated in the restaurant. When her coffee arrived, she cupped her hands around it, warming her fingers.

"With the flashlight, she went back out into the elements. The snow was already a foot deep, but the wind was still down. Nearby, there was a fallen tree that had been cleared from the road. She dragged pieces and parts of broken limbs toward the car and cleared a space in the road on the car's leeward side, where a fire would at least be partially sheltered from the wind. Beneath the branches, she stuffed smaller twigs and pine needles for kindling. There was a half-used matchbook in the glove compartment, and she went through all but the last four matches learning that the kindling was simply too wet to light on its own, much less to keep lit. From the back seat, she emptied the books from one of the boxes and tore off a piece of cardboard, which lit readily. Working the flame into the kindling set it to smoking. Before the first piece of the box burned out, she lit a second piece with the first, and used the second to light a third. The kindling finally caught and burned, though hissing and smoking from the moisture. Melting snow from the branches she attempted to add threatened the flame's life. A sudden, rising breeze extinguished it entirely.

"She turned on the flashlight again. The wind blew out the next match she lit. There were only two matches left. Leaning into the car as far as she could for shelter from the wind, she was able, with the next-to-last match, to light the last piece of the box, which she sheltered with her body while using it to re-light the fire.

"As she was deciding which box to empty next, her eye fell on one of the romance novels. On the cover was a semi-erotic illustration, the kind you see dozens of variations of on drugstore shelves—two seminude figures on the brink of succumbing to passion, with suggestive flames in the background. Flames? Sure, why not? She'd probably never get around to reading that one anyway, but she'd been almost too embarrassed to donate it to the library. She tore off the cover and watched as the printed flames sprang to life. The book's pages burned even better, balled and stuffed into the middle of the stack, the words of desire combusting, the lustful characters being consumed.

"The remainder of the book, when opened and fanned, burned quite nicely, and she sorted and selected more books, employing those of least value to her until the larger branches of wood were burning hotly enough to stay lit on their own.

"Her daughter was beginning to stir. After using a book of landscape photography to sweep the snow from around the fire, she hauled her suitcase out of the trunk to make a seat and stacked more wood within easy reach. She opened a bottle of wine—"

"Wait—she keeps a corkscrew in her car?"

"Of course. She's a fan of impromptu picnics, like the wonderfully romantic one you and I enjoyed on the beach last Saturday. Shall I continue?"

"Please."

"She lifted her daughter out of the car and brought her to the fire's warmth, wrapping the quilt around them both. Her pants were still wet, and she tried to keep her legs from shaking as she held and rocked her child on her lap, waiting, waiting for something, for anything, for the dawn if nothing else. The girl partly wakened and asked her mother where they were. Her mother reassured her that everything was all right. To help her fall asleep again, she told her one of their favorite stories, about a princess who, having been stranded on a tropical island, trained a troop of monkeys to help her survive in style.

"The fire was a boost to the mother's spirits, but it was hard for her to stave off the panic. She had brought only a few light snacks for her daughter. No one knew where they were. Her employer wasn't expecting her back to work for another two days and, knowing him, he might not bother to call the authorities for a week or two about her disappearance, if ever. If the wind picked up much more, she might not be able to keep the fire going for long—and she would have to sleep eventually regardless. Even if she could keep the fire lit, she would have to trek further and further through the deepening snow for usable wood. Eventually, regardless of the snow's depth, she'd probably have to try walking out, carrying her daughter.

"The snow began falling more heavily. She retrieved a compact umbrella from beneath her front seat, opened it and held it over them for protection, shaking off the snow's accumulation when it became heavy. Thinking about how she might go about fashioning of pair of snowshoes helped the time go by. As she was steeling herself for what might come and trying to decide on the right course of action, she was pleasantly shocked to see a pair of headlights coming down the hill toward them—"

"A police car."

"Yes. A county sheriff's deputy. She was wiping away tears of relief when the officer slowed to a stop beside her and asked what the trouble was. He had followed her tracks down from the top of the hill. The road should have already been gated, he said, and it certainly wouldn't be plowed. She explained her predicament. He tried to call someone on his radio, but it must have been out of range; the dispatcher could be heard talking, but the dispatcher couldn't hear him and he received no response. Of course he offered to give the woman and her child a ride out—insisted on it, informing her the current forecast indicated that the storm, despite the lull, was expected to last two or three days and that the worst was yet to come, and soon. He seemed nice enough, polite if a bit overly stern—like a certain detective I know, sometimes. Her daughter had awakened at his arrival and, not surprisingly, was enchanted by him, smiling at just about anything he said, no matter how seriously, reaching for him as she might have done for her father, had her father been around. The woman had no reason not to trust the officer. She thought that maybe he even found her attractive, by the way he looked her up and down while trying not to, smiling to himself a little when doing so. He did frown, though, when he saw the open bottle of wine.

"She asked if it would be at all possible, though she was very grateful for the offer of a ride, if instead he could siphon just a gallon or two of gas into her car, enough to get her up the hill and down to the next gas station. She really couldn't afford to lose her car and be without it for the winter. Once the snow got much deeper there would be no way to have it towed, and it might sit there all winter, through to the spring thaw. It could be June before she might be able to get it back, and by then it might need expensive repairs, if it could be made drivable at all.

"The deputy resisted, quoting this rule and that precedent, but she asked and asked, and asked again, as nicely and as sweetly and as charmingly as she could manage, practically begging. As it turned out, he did have a hose in his trunk. She had a bucket in hers that she had brought for cleaning. He finally relented, after making sure she understood how much of an exception he was making for her. He siphoned the gas into the bucket, and they poured it from the bucket into her tank, using a funnel she fashioned out of an old Time Life magazine from the magazine box.

"She was thanking him profusely for his help, for saving their lives, insisting that he and his wife or girlfriend, if he had either, should stop by her apartment for dinner or a drink whenever they might be down in town. He demurred, insisting that he was just doing his job. Noting the wine bottle again, he wanted to ensure that she was okay to drive. She showed him that she had had less than the equivalent of a glass, that she was just fine, truly. Seeing that he was cold and wet himself, from being out helping her, she offered to share some wine with him, suggesting he was welcome to stand or sit by the fire with her for a minute or two to warm himself before he left. Of course he had his own car to warm himself in, but it seemed the polite thing to offer. He took a respectable moment to consider it before insisting he didn't drink anymore, and certainly couldn't do so on duty anyway, and he had better be getting along. He was the most charming and helpful man, right up until the moment he spotted something in the edge of the fire that caught his attention.

"Something in the fire?"

"Yes—he bent down to look at something, and he asked her what it was. She wasn't sure what he was talking about. He got closer, picked up a stick and used it to flick something out of the fire's edge.

"'Oh, *that*,' she answered. She explained, rather proud of herself, that she had been using some of the books she was bringing back from Reno to get the fire started.

"'But what was *that* book,' he demanded. He seemed on the verge of being upset.

"She looked at it, squinted at it. On what was left of a charred, leather-bound cover was a line of embossed, gold-colored Arabic-looking script. 'Oh, *that*—that's probably just the cover of the Quran,' she told him."

"*The* Quran?" Frank asked. "You—*she* burned a *Quran*, and admitted doing so intentionally?"

"Funny," she answered, "that was pretty much the tone he used too. Sure, why not? It had thin pages—it burned readily. Besides, she didn't read Arabic, at least she was pretty sure that was the language it was written in. She wouldn't even have known what the book was except for a receipt in English that was tucked inside the front cover. The book was dog-eared, certainly not a collector's item, and if she ever wanted or needed to reference a Quran, she could either pick up an English translation for cheap at just about any bookstore or on the internet, if she needed a physical copy at all. The only reason she had included the volume in the milk crate with the other religious books was that she thought the letters on the spine were pretty and it might look nice filling out the religious section she envisioned for the reference shelf of her library."

"Pretty . . . Okay, but—"

"Frank, please."

"Jesus Christ—"

"Mohammed, actually," she said, smiling at herself. "But the deputy certainly wasn't happy. He was beside himself, angry by all indications. He asked if she knew that it was now against the law to burn a religious text, that only someone who lived under a rock wouldn't have heard of 'Penal Code number seventeen-something or other'. . . ."

"It's Penal Code Section 1705.4, the 'Religious Tolerance' statute passed last year. It makes it a felony, quote, 'to intentionally destroy, mutilate, mar, disfigure or alter in any way any symbol, building, text, image or object that is of established and central sacredness to any religious, faith-based or ideological group in a manner that would cause dishonor, defamation, offense, duress'—etc., etc."

"Well, it's just ridiculous, that's what it is, and she told the deputy so, that she couldn't believe that any upstanding American who had any respect whatsoever for the First Amendment and for free speech would want to enforce such a law, much less pay any mind to it."

"And *that* didn't go over well?"

"Apparently not. He went to his car, came back with a little plastic bag and, with a pair of tweezers, retrieved the burnt piece of the book cover. He put it in the bag and zipped it shut while lecturing her on respecting and obeying authority and the will of the majority and all laws whether she agreed with them or not. She countered that, at the very least, it was surely his job to exercise some discretion, that it would be the height of pettiness to be concerned about the fate of a Quran out in the middle of nowhere, in the middle of a winter storm, when two lives were at stake and there probably wasn't a Muslim within a hundred miles to be offended, and not a single Muslim in the whole country would ever know about her burning a Quran if he didn't choose to report it and make an issue of it—unless he was Muslim himself, of course."

"Assuming we're talking about the deputy I think we are, he certainly wasn't Muslim. He was a staunch Baptist."

"And that's what he said, but he claimed it was his responsibility to uphold the law, to protect the Muslims' sacred book whether he agreed with it or not, as surely as he would want a Muslim officer protecting the sacredness of the Bible, that at the very least she should have had the good sense and respect to burn every other book in the car and probably the seat covers too before she burned a Quran.

"She argued, in turn, that every other book in the car was likely of some great importance to someone in the world, to its author at the very least and maybe more so to the author's mother. She declared, moreover, that every other book in the car was simply of more value to her at the moment than the particular book in question, that the book was her property, and as such, she could do whatever she damned well pleased with it, regardless of its importance to anyone else, particularly considering that she was using it for keeping her and her daughter warm and alive, and frankly, she would have done the same damned thing if the Twelve Imams of Babcockistan had been standing right there watching her."

"The Twelve—who of where?"

"She just made that part up. She was trying to make a point."

"I gather." He glanced around. The only diners left in the restaurant were an older couple on the other side of the room, having dessert.

"And that's when he threatened to arrest her unless she could convince him that she was sorry. He said he might consider letting her off with a warning if he thought she were genuinely contrite and wouldn't think of doing such an incredibly thoughtless and stupid thing again. She was informed that it just so happened that his cousin was the county prosecutor, that his cousin's wife was best friends with the wife of the county judge, the very judge who would likely preside over her trial if she were charged, and he had it on good authority that the judge, being politically ambitious, would be more than eager to be the first in the state to oversee a verdict in such a case—the trial would probably be televised nationally—and the judge might be inclined to give the first person convicted under the statute the maximum penalty under law in order to set an example for anyone else who might be thinking of committing such defamation."

"The penalty is five to twenty years in prison, Elizabeth."

"That's exactly what the officer said. Well, she took it all in, looked him square in the eye and replied that if he were going to arrest her, he might as well dig around in the ashes and try to find evidence of the two Bibles she'd burned as well."

"Bibles? She burned—*Bibles*? Oh god . . ."

"Jesus Christ, this time." She smiled. "Yes, Bibles. Well, the deputy immediately started toeing and kicking at the fire with his boot, searching through the embers and ashes with his big flashlight. She said that there had been four or five Bibles, different versions and translations, in the milk crate in which she had packed the religious books. She wasn't yet sure which translations, if any, she might want to keep for reference, but when she needed more fuel for the fire, two of them were easily at hand, and she was even less likely to ever need all of the Bibles than she was to read some of the romance novels. Besides, as with the Quran, copies of the same editions could be picked up for a few dollars just about anywhere, so into the fire they had gone, along with an English translation of the Bhagavad Gita, which she had read back in college, out of curiosity, and was unlikely to ever read again. She explained all of this to the deputy."

Frank's mouth had opened but no words were forthcoming.

"The deputy said that the burning of the Bibles caused *him* great offense, that not only had she disrespected *his* faith, but the faith of millions of her fellow God-fearing Americans, that it hadn't been so long ago that she would have been burned at the stake, and rightly so, for such blasphemy.

"Her daughter, having reversed her opinion of the man, was crying. Holding the girl close, rocking her and trying to shush her, she countered to the deputy that in the milk crate there was at least one more Quran, probably three more Bibles, a Buddhist sutra and two Confucianism texts, and that if she ever found herself in the same circumstances again, she would burn every single one of them without a second thought or an ounce of guilt, particularly if doing so would provide her and her daughter with a few more hours of warmth. And furthermore—"

"There was a furthermore?"

"And furthermore, it would have been her right, once she got home, to make tiki torches out of every one of those books and to burn them for cheery light at a luau party if she wanted to—the books were *her* property, and she was an American, with her property rights protected under the Constitution of the United States of America, and that was that."

"And that was that. . . ."

"Yes, that was that. And that's when the deputy shined his flashlight squarely in her face and demanded she hand over her car key. His free hand was resting on the grip of his holstered pistol, his fingers tapping it impatiently. He had the gun—so she took the key off of her key ring and handed it to him. He turned on heel, marched over to his car and tried his radio again, almost yelling into it, but was still unable to raise a response. Pointing his finger at her, he told her that her attitude had just gotten her into a lot of trouble and that she was to extinguish the fire, cover the embers and find her license and registration while he was turning his car around. She tried to warn him that if he was going to try to turn around down at the hairpin turn to be careful because—but he had already slammed his door shut and was spinning his tires as he headed down.

"Well, when he reached the turn and got himself halfway turned around, sure enough, he ended up with his back wheels off in the same ditch, maybe even in the very same ruts that she had been stuck in. He gassed the engine and spun the tires, which only dug them in deeper, of course.

"The snow was beginning to fall in earnest again and the wind was picking up. She could hear his engine revving, the tires spinning, could see the car's lights pointing out over the side of the hill. Judging by the way he was going about it, she was fairly certain that it would only be a matter of time before he came walking back up the road in an even worse mood, that he'd arrest her, commandeer her car and drive the three of them up to the interstate where he could call for assistance.

"However, he hadn't yet arrested her, not officially, and he hadn't yet asked for any of her information. If there was a video camera on his car, it was probably blocked by snow. She couldn't go to jail. She just couldn't. There was no one else to take care of her daughter, and by dawn her daughter could end up being a ward of the state and would be put in foster homes for as many years as her mother might be incarcerated, possibly longer. Having been raised in foster homes herself, she was as willing to let that happen as she was to let her daughter freeze to death. Moreover, she had no intention of ending up in prison for having done what she deemed to be perfectly reasonable, logical, and moral, and she wasn't about to risk a judge or jury of any stripe deciding her fate on the weight of extenuating circumstances or political expediency. So she decided to leave."

"To leave? But she couldn't leave."

"She left. She hadn't been arrested yet. She hadn't done anything wrong. So she and her daughter left. End of story."

"That's not the end of the story."

"It's the end of my story." She exhaled. "Do you think we can still order dessert?"

Frank had already paid the bill. They hadn't seen the waiter in a while. He motioned the busser. When the young man came over, he was slipped a five-dollar bill and asked if he might be able to find them something sweet, preferably chocolate, in the kitchen.

"How did she leave? She walked out?"

"Oh my, no. She had a spare key in a magnetic holder beneath the bumper."

"I see." He thought for a moment. "But what is of more interest to me is what she left behind, and why."

"What do you mean?"

"He was found nine days later, you know."

"I noticed a report of it in the papers, yes."

"We left several details out of the news for purposes of the investigation."

"Oh?"

"Yes. For one, in the deputy's pocket, in an evidence bag, there was a piece of what I now believe to be the cover of a Quran, burnt around its edges. Only someone who had been there that night could have known about it."

"Yes . . ."

"I sent a couple of my guys back up there yesterday, now that the snow has melted. The only additional thing they discovered, lying in the road near where the deputy had been found, was this—" from his jacket pocket, he produced a car key—"The deputy may have dropped it or perhaps threw it in frustration."

"Oh . . ."

He extended it across the table for her to see. "I think we might know whose car this would start?"

"We might . . ."

He returned it to his pocket.

"There were several additional details that didn't get into the papers that perhaps you'd be interested in knowing."

"Okay . . ."

My Kingdom

"On that ninth day after the deputy disappeared, four days after the storm ended, a man was riding a snowmobile on the road below the antique shop, and he came across something odd. In the middle of the road were two pyramidal mounds of snow—a smaller one directly in front of a somewhat larger one. The rider stopped and, with his glove, brushed the snow off the smaller mound. It was a pyramid of books, all religious texts of one sort or another, all stood upright, all intact and partially fanned opened. Around the books were leaned twigs and branches, as if someone had set it up to start a fire. Oddly, there were ashes and charred pieces of wood on the pavement under the pile, as if there had already been a fire on that spot previously. When he brushed the snow off the larger mound next to the books, he found a man, frozen solid, sitting upright on a plastic milk crate, his eyes still open. He was wrapped in a pink unicorn blanket. There was an empty wine bottle on the ground beside him. In his left hand he held an empty matchbook. In his right hand, still clenched between his forefinger and thumb, was a single match, unused, unlit."

She said, "His car was still in the ditch, I assume."

"Buried beneath the snow. Out of gas. The battery dead."

With her spoon, she tried a bite of the chocolate cake.

"But he did have a match," she said.

"Indeed he did."

"And material with which to start a fire?"

"Arranged quite nicely."

"He even had a blanket and wine."

"Yes, generously."

"I hope he didn't have children."

"He left behind a wife and two children actually."

"That's a shame."

"It is."

She put the spoon down.

"I suppose, then, Detective Sullivan, that you're ready to wrap up your case."

"I'm wrapping it up now."

"You always get your man."

"Not always, but often enough."

They both sat erect, neither with the faintest trace of apology or regret in their bearing.

"Do you have any more questions for me, Frank?"

"I do."

"If you had asked sooner, I would have answered sooner, you know."

"I'm sure you would have, but I didn't have this key until yesterday. You do understand, Elizabeth, that if I have evidence in my possession that points to a crime having been committed, I'm obligated to turn it over to the district attorney in the jurisdiction where the crime occurred."

"You must do what you believe is right, Frank."

"I always do. And I will, but first, I want you to know that, even if your delivery was somewhat unconventional this evening, I understand why you presented it as you did, and I very much appreciate your forthrightness. I've come to expect nothing less of you."

"Thank you, Frank."

With that, he paused for a moment's consideration. Then he nodded his head decisively, withdrew a plastic bag from his jacket pocket, unsealed it and removed a singed scrap of leather with gold flame-shaped lettering on it. He examined the scrap, front and back, then lowered it deliberately to the candle on the table. The candle's flame grew as the scrap and the letters were consumed. When the fire reached his fingertips he dropped it in his coffee cup, where with a hiss and a curl of smoke, it ceased to be.

"In the case of the frozen deputy," he said, "I find that I have no evidence of a crime, nor in my considered judgment was any crime committed, except perhaps for the failure of the deceased to act appropriately and sufficiently on his own behalf."

He reached into his pocket, produced a car key and handed it to her.

"But—this isn't my key, Frank."

"It is your key, Elizabeth—your new key. You'll find that it starts your new car, which is waiting for you in the parking lot. It has four-wheel drive, all-weather tires, satellite radio, a roadside emergency kit, and a large gas tank."

"But Frank, I can't possibly accept—"

"You'll have to, Elizabeth. No wife of mine is going to be driving our children around in an unreliable, marginally safe vehicle."

"Frank?"

"I do have one more question for you this evening, Elizabeth."

He reached into his pocket.

"Oh, Frank . . ."

Short Plays

for stage & screen

QUENT CORDAIR

My Kingdom

NOTES FOR READERS

For those new to reading play scripts, the following notes on standard script formatting and direction may be helpful:

STAGE PLAYS

In scripts for stage plays, "(off)" indicates dialogue spoken from off stage.

SCREENPLAYS

In screenplays, scene descriptions are preceded by "INT," indicating "interior," if the scene is to be shot indoors, or "EXT," indicating "exterior," if the scene is outdoors. "EXT/INT" indicates both interior and exterior in the scene. Scene descriptions are followed by the time of day, e.g., "DAY" or "NIGHT."

In the first instance that a significant character is mentioned, the name will usually be in all caps. Sound effects may also be indicated in all caps.

"O.S." indicates that the dialogue is coming from "off screen"; "V.O." is "voice over"; "(filtered)" is commonly used to indicate voice coming over a radio or phone. "POV" as a camera angle indicates "point of view."

QUENT CORDAIR

"AN UNCOMFORTABLE SILENCE"

A short stage play

Cast of Characters

<u>Him</u>: A man in his mid-20s to mid-30s.

<u>Her</u>: A woman in her mid-20s to mid-30s.

Time

The present.

Scene

A domestic sitting-room.

<u>Setting</u>: Two chairs, at 45-degrees to downstage, with (optionally) side tables, a reading lamp, coffee table. A coat rack with his and her coats nearer the exit.

<u>At rise</u>: The couple is sitting silently. He's distractedly trying to read a news magazine. She's restlessly shifting between a fashion magazine and flipping through social media on her phone. They're palpably upset with each other. Uncomfortably, there's

                    no talk at all for nearly the first
                    full minute, though each is fully
                    aware of, attuned to, each sound and
                    shift and page turn made by the
                    other, while trying to mask it;
                    attempting, unsuccessfully, to
                    project their own detachment and
                    lack of concern.

                              HIM
Ready to go to dinner?

                              HER
Whenever.

                              HIM
Not hungry?

                              HER
I could take it or leave it.

                    (Her phone rings.)

                              HER
                         (into phone)
Hi, Mom.... Yes ... No ... I don't know ...
Probably ... I know, I'm sorry. Can we talk
later?... No, it's fine ... We're fine ... I
know, but – can we talk later? We're headed out
to dinner.... I'll call you later, or in the
morning, okay?... Thanks ... Love you, too. Bye.

                    (More silence. More attempted
                    reading.)

                              HER
I'm going out for a walk.

                    HIM
Okay.

          (She gets up, puts phone in
          coat pocket, starts to take
          coat, stops and turns.)

                    HER
I'm leaving.

          (He looks at her, says nothing.
          She starts to take her coat
          again, stops and turns.)

                    HER
               (lightly, laughing)
Okay, this is just ridiculous.

                    Him
               (relieved)
I couldn't agree more. Ridiculous!

                    HER
Did you enjoy that at all?

                    HIM
No! How on earth is that supposed to be enjoyable?

                    HER
But our friends say that it makes things, you know, spicier - when they make up.

                    HIM
You think it could be spicier for us?

                    HER
I'm not sure I could stand spicier.

                    HIM
Well, we tried it.

          (She goes to him.)

                    HER
We never fight. Let's never fight again. Even in
play. That was horrible.

                    HIM
Horrible, yes. Never again.

          (They kiss.)

                    HER
It was frightening, really.

                    HIM
Frightening? Oh, I'm sorry. If I had known it was
frightening to you, I'd have called an end to it
on the spot.

                    HER
You weren't frightened?

                    HIM
I wouldn't say frightened. It was starting to
worry me though. It was bordering on fearful.

                    HER
It seemed pretty real to me. As though you were
actually angry with me. Truly angry.

                    HIM
You seemed genuinely upset yourself. I thought
maybe you were really about to walk out on me
there.

HER
You really thought I would?

HIM
My heart was starting to break a little. It felt real.

HER
I'm sorry.

(She comes to him again.)

HIM
I'm sorry too.

(They kiss again.)

HER
Never again?

HIM
Never again. Let's go to dinner.

(She goes to get her coat again, with him following. She stops and turns to him.)

HER
What was your reason?

HIM
My reason?

HER
We had reasons, didn't we? We agreed to come up with pretend reasons, so we could better pretend we were upset. What was your reason?

                              HIM
I'd rather not say.

                              HER
Oh, come on. It wasn't real. You can tell me.
What was it? Had I cheated on you or something?

                              HIM
No! You would never ... I couldn't even pretend
that.

                              HER
Of course I would never. But what <u>could</u> you
pretend?

                              HIM
Do we do have to do this? Let's just let it go.
Let's go to dinner and forget about it.

                              HER
We can go to dinner.... But we promised we'd tell
each other our reasons.

                              HIM
We did?

                              HER
We did. And we always keep our promises, don't
we?

                              HIM
Of course. We always keep our promises.

                              HER
And?

                              HIM
I'd still rather not say.

HER
But you promised. Why would you want to keep it from me? Is it something you think I could actually do?

HIM
No. Not really. I mean, not unless ...

HER
So you do think I'm capable of it.

HIM
But, you wouldn't.

HER
What wouldn't I do?

HIM
Please. I can't tell you. Not now.

HER
But we promised. What's wrong? You can't trust me with something? If it's something I might do wrong, enough to upset you as much as you were upset, I want to know about it. We're too important to me. Please?

HIM
You won't be upset?

HER
How could I be upset? I haven't actually done anything!

HIM
You could be upset that I think you're capable of it.

                    HER
Well, maybe I am. If you think I am, I probably
am. Now what the hell is it?

                    HIM
See, you're getting upset.

                    HER
Because you won't tell me!

                    HIM
And you'll tell me your reason?

                    HER
I promised, didn't I?

                    HIM
You go first then.

                    HER
            (exasperated)
Fine!
            (she thinks about it)
I can't.

                    HIM
Oh, are you kidding me?

                    HER
See, now you're upset too.

                    HIM
What could I possibly do that would make you want
to walk out on me like that?

                    HER
But I didn't walk out.

HIM
You were about to.

HER
Well, if you had —

HIM
If I had what?

(She doesn't reply.)

HIM
Can we just go to dinner?

HER
I think we need to clear this up before we go anywhere.

HIM
I don't want to lose you.

HER
How could you lose me?

HIM
It's what I fear most. Losing you.

HER
So don't do anything that might drive me away.

HIM
So there *is* something —

HER
But you wouldn't actually do it though — would you?

                    HIM
I don't even know what it is! I didn't know there
was something I could do that could make you
leave. Are you going to tell me?

                    HER
I can't....

                    HIM
You don't care about us enough to tell me?

                    HER
Oh, you did not just go there!

                    HIM
I'm sorry. I didn't mean it that way.

                    HER
I think maybe you did.

                    HIM
What are we doing?

                    HER
We're afraid. We're both afraid. We're too
afraid. This isn't working.

                    HIM
Let's make it work then. We have to make it work.
What can I do?

                    HER
You can tell me. Whatever it is. What were you
pretending I had done that made you so upset with
me?

                    HIM
This wasn't the way it was supposed to happen.

          (She's confused. She waits.
          He decides.)

                    HIM
You had said "no."

                    HER
"No"?

                    HIM
You said "no."

                    HER
I said "no" to what?

                    HIM
This wasn't supposed to happen until at least after dinner - or sometime, someday....

                    HER
What wasn't supposed to happen?

                    HIM
I was going to ask you something. And you said "no."

                    HER
And that made you angry?

                    HIM
More hurt really. Really hurt.

                    HER
I would never want to hurt you. I'm so sorry....

                    HIM
I know you wouldn't. And you didn't. You haven't.
It would have hurt you to hurt me, and I wouldn't
ever want to put you in that position. It
wouldn't be fair. And so — I wouldn't. I won't.

                    HER
Put me in what position?

                    HIM
In a position to have to say "no."

                    HER
Why would I have to say "no"?

                    HIM
Because you've always said you'd never want that
again. Not after your last. That you want to
remain free from now on, uncommitted, for your
own protection. That you don't ever want to be
hurt that badly again.

                    HER
Oh ... But you wouldn't hurt me.

                    HIM
Wouldn't I? Isn't that what you were pretending
I'd done? Hurt you somehow? If it wasn't that,
what?

                    HER
Do I have to tell you?

                    HIM
You promised.

                    HER
We always keep our promises....

                    HIM
We always keep our promises.

                    HER
I imagined that I had overheard you tell your
mother something.

                    HIM
What?

                    HER
That you were never going to ask me.

                    HIM
Why would I never ask?

                    HER
I don't know. Maybe you didn't want me enough.
Maybe I wasn't worth the risk.

                    HIM
The risk of what?

                    HER
The risk of hearing me say "no."

                    HIM
You're impossible.

                    HER
We're impossible.

                    HIM
Impossibly in love.

                    HER
In love enough?

>   (Long pause. He decides.
>   Reaches into his pocket,
>   retrieves a ring, slowly lowers
>   to one knee, takes her hands.)
>   HIM
> In love enough to hear you say "no" every day for
> the rest of my life, as long as you'll let me
> keep asking, as long as you'll not walk out the
> door. Not without me.
>   HER
> Keep asking what?
>
>   HIM
> Will you marry me?
>
>   HER
> No fighting?
>
>   HIM
> Not even pretend.
>
>   HER
> We'll always keep our promises?
>
>   HIM
> We'll always keep our promises.
>
>   HER
> Even if I say "no"?
>
>   HIM
> Even if you say "no."
>
>   HER
> Ask me again.

MY KINGDOM

              HIM

Will you marry me?

              HER

I promise.

        (He puts the ring on her finger. They embrace, kiss. He lifts and spins her around.)

              HIM

Dinner?

              HER

Anything you want.

        (They exit, arm in arm, gazing into each other's eyes. They've forgotten their coats. He dashes back in for them.)

              HER
        (off)

I'm calling my mother!

              (END)

MY KINGDOM

"SILVER ANGEL"

A short screenplay

FADE IN:

INT. BAR - DAY

A hot summer day in a roadside bar. The ceiling fans whirl lazily as COUNTRY MUSIC plays quietly on the jukebox. The bar is empty except for ANNIE, the bartender, an attractive, intelligent, single woman. During the second verse, the song playing on the jukebox skips, the music sputters and stops, the jukebox flickering and going out. Annie shakes her head, used to it.

A MOTORCYCLE is heard approaching, slowing, coming to a stop, idling, turning off. A BIKER walks in, confident, at ease, well-groomed, handsome with a rugged edge, wears a leather riding jacket, boots, jeans. Looks around. The place seems all right. The bartender seems more than all right. She's attracted to him too, but warily. He walks past her, sits at the end of the bar farthest from door. She follows.

                    ANNIE
          What will it be?

                    BIKER
          Water, please.

She raises an eyebrow but pours and brings him
the water. He finishes it in one long, slow
drink. She regards him questioningly.

                    BIKER
          A good bourbon, rocks.

She pours, places it in front of him. From his
pocket he retrieves an antique silver lighter and
studies the engraved angel on it. She goes to put
an ashtray in front of him but he shakes his
head. She takes the ashtray away. He flicks the
lighter, studies the flame. Sips the whiskey,
approves. She starts wiping down the back bar,
dusting and straightening the bottles, stealing
glances through the mirror.

A TRUCK is heard pulling into the lot. The truck
door CLOSES more loudly than necessary. A new
customer, RUDY, a large, brash man, enters, looks
around. Neither Annie nor the biker recognize
him. Rudy strolls to the center of the bar,
noisily pulls out a barstool and sits.

                    RUDY
          Whatever ya got on tap will
          be great, darlin'. And a
          nice cold glass too if
          you've got one. Hot day,
          isn't it?

                    ANNIE
          It's been hotter.

As she bends to get a chilled glass out of the lower cooler, he openly checks out her assets and glances at the biker, smiling. Biker ignores him. Rudy resumes checking out Annie.

>   RUDY
>   Nice...

She flashes him a look of warning, as politely as she can manage.

>   RUDY
>   Nice...place you've got
>   here.

He gets no response from her. He looks around.

>   RUDY
>   Just passing through.
>   Thinking I might stay the
>   night around here
>   somewhere. What's a
>   handsome fellow with some
>   cash to burn supposed to do
>   for distraction in these
>   parts?

>   ANNIE
>   Got a book?

>   RUDY
>   That's good. Good...

Biker is quietly amused. Rudy is undeterred. He takes a long drink from his beer while studying her. Checks to make sure there's no competition from the biker.

                    RUDY
          People have to eat, ya
          know. How about a big
          steak-and-wine dinner on me
          this evening? Wherever you
          wanna go, hun. I'll treat
          ya like a queen.

                    ANNIE
          Thanks, but I have plans.

                    RUDY
          You have plans...

He glances at the biker; the biker remains unreadable.

                    RUDY
          Well maybe my plan's
          better. Come on, darlin',
          what da ya say?

She nods at his wedding ring.

                    ANNIE
          Why don't we check with
          your wife and see what she
          thinks about your plans?

                    RUDY
          Ya didn't have to bring her
          into it, now, did ya?

                    ANNIE
          I didn't, but I did.

He drains his beer and taps the empty glass, ready for another. She retrieves the glass and begins to put it under the tap.

                    RUDY
          I'll take a fresh glass.

She pauses, collects herself, bends down to get
another glass from the cooler. Rudy enjoys seeing
what he sees. The biker flicks the cigarette
lighter and watches the flame, both Rudy and
Annie taking note. Annie pours and delivers the
beer then eases her way down to the biker. His
glass is only half empty.

                    ANNIE
               (hopefully)
          Is there anything more I
          can do for you?

                    BIKER
          Not yet, thanks.

She looks for something to do on his end, not
wanting to return to the middle of the bar. She
finds the remote and turns on the TV. A menu
comes up. She starts scrolling through it. Rudy
is studying her intently.

                    RUDY
          Hey -

She ignores him. Rudy is still staring, trying to
figure something out, trying to remember...

                    RUDY
          Hey!

He motions her to him with his finger.
Reluctantly she returns.

                    RUDY
          You know, I'm starting to
          think I might know you from
          somewhere. Haven't quite
          been able to put my finger
          on it, but I'm almost sure
          of it... You ever been down
          Cumberland County way?

                    ANNIE
               (after a beat)
          I've been to a lot of
          places.

At the mention of Cumberland County, she has
become very uncomfortable, concerned, though she
tries to hide it. Turns slightly away to shift
some glasses around so that he doesn't have so
clear a view. He finishes half the beer and wipes
his mouth on his sleeve.

                    RUDY
          But I've seen you. You got
          relatives down our way
          maybe, in Cumberland
          County? You visited lately?

                    ANNIE
          I have relatives in a lot
          of places. Cumberland
          County is a very long way
          from here. Now is there a
          baseball game on or
          something you might like to
          watch?

> RUDY
> I have better things to
> watch than a ballgame.
> (finishes beer) And I'll
> have another.

She goes to refill the glass.

> RUDY
> In another cold glass.

She shakes her head but bends to get it.

> BIKER
> - please.

Rudy glances his way. Biker is studying his lighter, flicks the flame.

> BIKER
> Please. You'd like another
> cold glass - please.

Rudy assesses him, sizing him up. Finally he laughs, too loudly.

> RUDY
> What the man says. He's
> right - where are my
> manners? Do you think I'm
> being rude, darlin'?

She serves his beer.

> ANNIE
> Probably just the way you
> were raised.

                    RUDY
          Yeah, we're probably not
          quite as sophisticated in
          Cumberland County as folks
          up in these parts. But I
          know I've seen you. Wait -
          weren't you at that
          barbeque that the Dolittles
          threw on the 4th a couple
          years ago? Yes, you were...
          My wife and I were sittin'
          at the same table as - wait
          a minute...

He's studying her hard. She's becoming very
concerned. Turns to clean the backbar to keep her
face turned away from him entirely.

                    RUDY
          No, turn around here,
          darlin'. Let me see you.

In desperation, she accidentally-on-purpose
knocks a glass to the floor. It breaks. Bending
low, she turns away from him to pick up the
pieces.

                    RUDY
          Now, now. You know I like
          this view, darlin', but you
          just stand right back up
          here and let me see your
          face.... Come on, now.

Slowly, she rises. She turns to face him.

                    ANNIE
          You don't know me...

> RUDY
> Oh, but I think I do.
> You're ... You're Tom
> Shelly's wife, aren't you.
> Yes, you are. The one who
> ran away awhile back.
> Changed your hair maybe.
> See, you can't even bring
> yourself to deny it. From
> what I hear, ol' Tom's
> still damned upset about it
> too, been lookin' all over
> the place for you. Imagine,
> runnin' into you all the
> way up here.

She's dismayed.

> ANNIE
> Look, I don't know you. I
> don't remember you, but you
> must be a decent man. There
> are plenty of people in
> town who will vouch for me,
> who know what he used to do
> to me, and the restraining
> order didn't slow him down
> one bit. You can't tell him
> where I am now. You can't.

> RUDY
> Maybe I can't. Maybe I can.

He's starting to get an idea.

> RUDY
> A man has a right to know
> where his wife is, I
> figure.

The biker flicks the lighter.

>   ANNIE
> I moved a few towns away,
> hoping that would be
> enough. But he tracked me
> down. I have the scars to
> show for it. I finally
> found this place, this job
> - it's not much, but it's
> what I have. Please be
> decent and leave me be.
>
>   RUDY
> Oh, I can be decent. I can
> be as decent as somebody's
> willing to be decent to me
> in turn. Now as I recall,
> when I came in here I
> generously offered a lady
> the opportunity to enjoy a
> nice meal and an evening of
> conversation - and I got
> nothing but a cold shoulder
> in return. How decent was
> that? Oh, and I'll be
> having another beer. In a
> cold glass -

- glances challengingly at the biker. The biker sips his whiskey, looking straight ahead -

> RUDY
> Now, I'm thinking that somebody might be willing to be a little more decent to somebody else this evening if she wants some decency in return. And I'm thinking I might be coming back through this way on my travels on a more regular basis to enjoy a little more of a certain lady's decency. Whadaya say? -

> ANNIE
> Please...

She glances to the biker. He's examining the lighter, running his thumb over the engraved angel.

> RUDY
> Well, it's up to you, darlin'. (Pulls out his phone) Now, I don't think I have Tom's number myself, but my buddy Dave plays golf with him fairly regularly. Dave will probably have his number.... (starts searching contacts)

Biker gets up deliberately and walks toward him. Rudy, thinking there's going to be a confrontation, begins to turn to defend himself, but the biker brushes by him and walks out, the door shutting behind him.

Annie despairs at seeing the biker go. Rudy smiles, pleased to have Annie to himself. Running out of options, she reaches towards Rudy's phone, hoping to stop or delay him somehow.

> ANNIE
> Please...

> RUDY
> Well, I think I'm beginning to sense a more reasonable attitude now. I'm not a bad guy, you know. I just need a little attention sometimes, like any other man.

He takes her by the wrist.

> ANNIE
> Just dinner.

> RUDY
> Sure, just dinner. We'll talk. Get to know each other. My name's Rudy, by the way. What was yours again? Ellen? Amanda? Abby?

> ANNIE
> Annie. Promise me - Rudy - that it's just dinner. Just dinner and talk.

                    RUDY
          Annie, somebody's starting
          to sound a little rude and
          unreasonable again, and I
          haven't even begun to be
          bad to you yet. Don't ya
          think a little tit for tat
          would be only fair? I mean,
          if this is the way you were
          treatin' ol' Tom, I'm
          starting to see how he
          might have taken offense -

He pulls her in closer, almost close enough to
kiss. Runs a finger down her jawline, starts to
try to trace her lower lip as she tries to pull
back. Biker comes back in, finishing a text on
his phone. Sees what's happening at the bar. Puts
phone in pocket as he walks up very close, then
sits on the barstool immediately next to Rudy,
away from the door.

                    BIKER
               (to Annie)
          When you have a moment,
          ma'am, if I could have
          another drink, and another
          beer for our friend here -
          please.

With Rudy distracted, Annie twists out of his
grip, relieved momentarily but upset. Tries to
maintain her poise. She serves them both. Rudy is
uncomfortable with the new situation, with the
biker sitting nearly shoulder to shoulder. Both
men sit in silence and sip their drinks. Biker's
phone DINGS a notification. He checks a text,
nods.

> BIKER
> That your truck in the lot?

> RUDY
> I don't think there's another.

> BIKER
> License number MX0743L?

> RUDY
> What of it?

> BIKER
> That would make you Mr. Rudolph Estes Pisselman.

> RUDY
> The name is Rudy.

> BIKER
> Mr. Rudolph Estes Pisselman, of 1832 Sweetwater Drive, Oakvale. Birthday, February 27th, '75.

Rudy sips his beer. He's not happy. Biker sets his phone and the lighter on the bar. Silence between the men. Moments pass. Biker's phone DINGS again. He checks it.

> BIKER
> In sales for Tri-State Combine? Solid company. On the road a lot, I suppose. (scrolls through text) Guessing the company probably isn't aware of those two DUIs yet....

Rudy begins to steam, trying to decide what to do. Both men take a drink. Uncomfortable silence. The biker flicks the lighter again. Biker's phone DINGS again. He checks it.

> BIKER
> I suppose Mrs. Pisselman is unaware of those charges on your credit card from Brown's Valley Ranch — that little place up the way here that you like to visit when you're through. Those charges aren't exactly for purchases of beef, are they, Rudolph? So, does the ranch charge by the pound for the kind of flesh they serve up over there, or - ?

Rudy jumps up and takes a swing, but the biker coolly has Rudy in a hammerlock and leaned hard over the bar before he can blink. Biker forcefully helps Rudy sit back down, all without his own temper rising a single degree. Sits down again himself.

> BIKER
> Careful there, Rudolph. You almost spilled your beer. We wouldn't want to do that now, would we? Would you like another?

Rudy shakes his head. Biker has another slow sip of his drink, studies his lighter, then turns directly to face Rudy and scoots in very close, lighter in hand so that Rudy sees what's on it, bringing his face within inches of Rudy's.

                    BIKER
          Ever heard of the Silver
          Angels, Rudolph?

Rudy shakes his head.

                    BIKER
          Ever seen a man die slowly
          in the desert after having
          all his limbs broken, bones
          protruding from the skin,
          scorpions stuffed in his
          mouth, lips taped shut,
          body left exposed for the
          buzzards to pick clean...

Rudy jumps up, knocking over his barstool and
runs for the door, tries to open it but discovers
that the biker has slid the bolt shut. Swears
under his breath and struggles to wiggle the bolt
open, but the biker is right behind him,
uncomfortably close again, his hand holding the
door shut.

                    BIKER
          Rudolph, I trust that
          you've already forgotten
          who the bartender here is
          (Rudy nods), that you've
          forgotten where she is
          (Rudy nods), and you'll be
          detouring well around this
          town anytime you might ever
          have cause to be in the
          area again, or - (his phone
          DINGS again) - My
          apologies, Rudolph. Excuse
          me for a moment.

Checks his phone with his other hand, shakes his head in wonder.

>   BIKER
>   You know, a married man
>   should never let his photo
>   be taken with Miss Brandy
>   down at Brown's Ranch, not
>   in that position... Not
>   your best look, Rudolph.

Glancing at his phone again, he squints, winces with bemusement, glances down at Rudy's crotch, shakes his head apologetically.

Rudy is mortally embarrassed. Biker finally releases the door, opens it for Rudy. Rudy departs hastily. Gravel can be HEARD beneath spinning tires. Biker returns to bar, sits down to finish his drink. Annie is relieved, grateful, attracted strongly to the biker, though now he seems too dangerous. Yet...

>   ANNIE
>   Mind if I ask how you found
>   out all of that about him?

>   BIKER
>   Called in a couple of
>   favors from friends in law
>   enforcement and tech
>   security. I expect Rudy
>   won't be using his birthday
>   as his password on
>   everything anymore.

He takes another drink of his whiskey. She hesitates.

                    ANNIE
          Have you ever left someone
          to die in the desert that
          way?

Biker shakes his head.

                    ANNIE
          Ever watched someone else
          do it?

                    BIKER
          I read a scene like that in
          a novel once. Sounded
          pretty nasty, didn't it?

                    ANNIE
          That was an impressive move
          you put on him.

                    BIKER
          Our college judo team made
          it to nationals. It still
          comes in handy now and
          then.

She glances at the lighter, back at him.

                    BIKER
          Picked it up at an antique
          store this morning. Nice,
          isn't it?

                    ANNIE
          You're not with a gang of
          some kind?

                    BIKER
          Investment banker, out on
          the road for a few days to
          get some fresh air and
          enjoy the views.

He glances at her appreciatively.

                    ANNIE
          There are no Silver Angels
          then?

He finishes his drink.

                    BIKER
          I wouldn't go that far.

He lays a large bill on the bar and starts to go.
She's surprised, disappointed he's leaving.

                    ANNIE
          Please, it's on me.

                    BIKER
          A tip then, thanks.

He begins walking out.

                    ANNIE
          Thank you.

He turns.

                    BIKER
          You're welcome.

He continues walking out.

                    ANNIE
          I hope I'll see you again.

He turns, smiles, turns and walks out, silhouetted against the light outside. Sound of the MOTORCYCLE being kick-started, pulling out, shifting through the gears, heading down the highway.

She begins wiping down the bar. Goes to remove his glass and realizes that he's left the lighter. She picks it up, lets her thumb caress the engraved angel. She pockets it in her apron and smiles. As she comes around the end of the bar to straighten the barstools, she gives the jukebox a nudge in passing. The SONG starts up again where it had left off. The ceiling fans spin slowly above.

FADE OUT:

THE END

My Kingdom

QUENT CORDAIR

MY KINGDOM

"MUJAHID"

A short screenplay

FADE IN:

INT. HUSAM'S BEDROOM - NIGHT (PRE-DAWN)

HUSAM, 17, lies awake in the dark, staring at the ceiling. The ALARM on his phone goes off — it's the morning call to PRAYER, in Arabic. He gets out of bed and kneels on the rug, head to floor, to pray.

INT. HALL - DAY (DAWN)

Husam emerges from his bedroom and waits in the hall for his sister to emerge from the bathroom. She's SINGING along to American pop MUSIC. He bangs on the bathroom door impatiently. FARAH, 16, finally emerges, dressed fashionably, attractively, in tight jeans, form-fitting top, make-up.

                    HUSAM
          If you tried to go out of
          the house like that and
          father were here, he would
          beat you.

                    FARAH
          Well he's not here, is he.

                    HUSAM
          Maybe I should beat you
          myself.

                    FARAH
          Maybe you should have
          tracking chips installed in
          your balls so you can find
          them in the lake the day
          you lay a hand on me.

Husam curses quietly in Arabic as he brushes past
her -

                    HUSAM
          Assumu-alaikum ... ("Death
          be upon you")

                    FARAH
          Wa alaika assamu wa la'na
          ... ("Death to you too, and
          be damned on top of it.")

INT. JASIM'S BEDROOM - DAY (DAWN)

Through the open door of his bedroom, JASIM, 9,
their younger brother, smiles approvingly at
Farah as she passes. She smiles back, winks at
him. On the walls of Jasim's room are posters of
superheroes, Chicago Cubs baseball, sports cars,

sailboats cutting through waves on the lake. He practices tying a sailor's knot on a length of rope while watching a video tutorial on a tablet.

                    MOTHER (O.S.)(calling)
    Kids, breakfast...

INT. KITCHEN - DAY

MOTHER, late-30s, beautiful though careworn, is listening to the radio as she puts breakfast on the table, preparing lunches, cleaning the kitchen as she goes.

                    FEMALE RADIO VOICE
                    (V.O.)(filtered)
    ...the accident should be cleared on the Eisenhower shortly; the Skyway, the Jane Adams and the Reagan are rolling at the speed limit; the Tri-State and Veterans expressways are looking good as well. From the Chicagoland Weather Center, some flurries at times near the lake today with a high of 35. Tomorrow, partly sunny and a high of 36. Presently 34 at O'Hare. Midway, 37. Evanston, 34. 35 at Chicago's lakefront with the barometer on the rise. That's WJN Traffic & Weather. Bob?

>   MALE RADIO VOICE
>   (V.O.)(filtered)
> Thanks, Robin. From the WJN
> News Center this morning:
> despite the unsolved
> explosions two weeks ago
> that killed two and wounded
> thirteen, holiday
> decorations are going up
> downtown and festivities
> are in full swing along the
> Magnificent Mile and around
> the Loop. Police Chief
> Joseph Adams says that
> extra precautions will be
> in place today, but plans
> are to go ahead with the
> tree lighting in Daley
> Plaza this evening....

Mother turns down the volume as Farah enters with her book bag, greeting her mother with a kiss before sitting at the table.

>   MOTHER
> Please stay away from
> downtown today, Farah.

>   FARAH (shrugging)
> Sure, Mom ...

>   MOTHER
> Husam, Jasim! Breakfast!
> Now!

The news has segued to HOLIDAY/CHRISTMAS MUSIC.

MY KINGDOM

INT. JASIM'S BEDROOM - DAY

Jasim puts his tablet in his backpack and the backpack over his shoulder. He exits his room while practicing the sailor's knot again; nearly runs into Husam in the hall.

INT. HALL - DAY

>   HUSAM
>   You waste your time on
>   foolish things, Jasim.

Husam tugs the end of the rope; the knot comes undone; he shakes his head dismissively.

>   JASIM
>   That's what that one is
>   supposed to do.

Jasim reties the knot as he follows Husam into the kitchen.

INT. KITCHEN - DAY

The boys join Farah at the table. Husam is sullen, distracted. Jasim, eager for the day, eats voraciously.

>   JASIM
>   Can we go sailing today,
>   Farah?

                    FARAH
          It's too cold now, Jasim.
          Freddy's boat has been
          hauled out for the winter
          already.

                    JASIM
          But Freddy said I could be
          his first mate when I've
          learned my knots. I've
          learned my knots.

                    FARAH
          Maybe in the spring, Jasim.

                    JASIM
          Can we go downtown today,
          Husam?

Husam is distracted by his phone beneath the
table.

                    MOTHER
          You have school today,
          Jasim. Husam, please eat.

                    JASIM
          But school is boring. I
          already know everything
          they're teaching.

                    MOTHER
          I'm sorry, Jasim - you have
          to go to school.

JASIM
But I want to go downtown and see the tree and all the decorations in the windows.

MOTHER
I have to go. Please put your phone away, Husam. You haven't touched your breakfast.

HUSAM
Mother, you should at least have the decency to cover your head when you go out.

MOTHER
You're hanging out with the wrong people, Husam. If you're not careful, you're going to end up like your father.

HUSAM
I would be so honored, inshallah.

MOTHER
And I don't want your new "friends" in the house again. Do you hear me? If you're not going back to school, I want you to look for a job today. And not just look – get a job. There's work to be found if you want it. It's time to start being responsible.

                    HUSAM (mutters in Arabic)
                Tawakkal-tu-'ala-Allah...
                ("I have put my faith in
                Allah")

                    MOTHER
                English, Husam. I have to
                go. Make sure Jasim gets on
                the school bus today.

                    JASIM
                Why do I have to go to
                school if Husam doesn't?

                    MOTHER
                You're going to school,
                Jasim.

She goes around the table and kisses her
children. Husam leans away from her.

                    MOTHER
                Husam, please stay out of
                trouble today. Please...

Mother exits as Farah's boyfriend, FREDDY, 18,
arrives to pick Farah up for school. He HONKS
politely to get her attention.

                    MOTHER
                Farah, Freddy's here.

Farah grabs her book bag and hurriedly follows
her mother out. Jasim goes to the window. Freddy
waves from his new Mercedes convertible.

JASIM
Oh my god! He got it. He got the SLK-350!

HUSAM
Let me guess – you want one just like it.

JASIM
No, mine will be blue, just like the sails on my boat....

HUSAM
Only murtadds and kafirs lust after such things, little brother. Farah's kafir boyfriend is rich.

JASIM
Then I'll be rich too.

HUSAM
Our sister has become a kafir's whore. Falling prey to worldly temptations and desires for worldly wealth – it is against the will of Allah. You must learn to seek after spiritual things, little brother, to think only of treasures in heaven.... How would you make that kind of money anyway?

JASIM
I don't know. I'll figure it out.

Husam becomes absorbed in texting on his phone.

                    HUSAM
          Don't miss the bus, Jasim.

                    JASIM
          I want to go downtown,
          Husam. Please?

                    HUSAM (distracted)
          Not today, Jasim. Not today
          of all days ... Hurry,
          you'll be late.

                    JASIM
          Why not today? What's wrong
          with today?

                    HUSAM
          Get out of here. Go on now.
          Go.

Jasim reluctantly dons his Cubs jacket, collects
his book bag and lunch. Grabs an extra pudding
cup out of the refrigerator. Husam checks his
watch, continues texting. He studies his phone
screen with growing concern and confusion as
Jasim heads towards front door and exits. Husam
goes to the front window and scans the street.

EXT. RESIDENTIAL STREET, CHICAGO - DAY

The school bus approaches. Jasim glances back to
check the front window of the modest brownstone:
Husam is texting again, not watching. The school
bus passes, slowing to a stop nearby. Rather than
hurrying to catch the bus, as he easily could,
Jasim purposefully misses it. Dodging traffic, he

crosses the street to wait at a CTA (Chicago Transit Authority) bus stop, tucking around the side to stay out of his brother's sight.

From the window, Husam recognizes a BEARDED MAN, late-20s, approaching the house, carrying a relatively heavy, though not large, black backpack. Husam lets him in the house, glancing both ways along the street. From the bus stop, Jasim watches the two interact through the brownstone's front window. The man hurriedly explains something. Husam, at first, seems taken aback; shakes his head protesting, but shortly, at the man's insistence and encouragement, Husam relents and agrees. The man gives Husam the backpack and urgent, final instructions, gesturing regarding the pack and its contents. The man checks his watch, they exchange an Islamic State salute (index-finger raised) followed by brushing kisses.

The bearded man leaves the house as a CTA bus approaches the stop at which Jasim waits. Husam exits the house hurriedly and dashes across the street with the black backpack.

INT/EXT BUS - DAY - TRAVELING

The public-transit bus, with the typical two doors on the same side, front and rear, is lightly occupied. Jasim has already boarded and taken a seat near the rear, next to the window, right side, when Husam boards. When Jasim sees him, he ducks low. Husam takes a seat closer to the front, left side, window.

Husam begins silently praying, glancing in near disbelief at the backpack that he has set on the floor between his legs. He checks the other passengers as casually as he can. They eye him in turn, as casually as they can. Despite the one man across the aisle who seems suspicious, no one says anything.

Jasim, relieved that he hasn't been seen, relaxes as the bus pulls away. He begins to enjoy the ride, the views. He's in his element, exploring the city, the big adventure, soaking in all that an ambitious, life-loving boy would: the interesting buildings, well-dressed women and men, nice cars, skylines, architecture, fast trains, luxury stores, restaurant windows, food trucks.... His expression is all wonderment and expectation.

With his nose and forehead plastered to the glass, he hasn't noticed that Husam has come back to sit down next to him. When he does notice, he knows that he's in trouble, but he remains determined, undefeated.

                HUSAM
     You have to go home, Jasim.

Jasim turns away, continues looking through the window.

                HUSAM
     You have to get off at the
     next stop and take the next
     bus home.

Jasim doesn't respond.

                    HUSAM
          You're going to be in so
          much trouble if I have to
          tell mom.

Husam gets out his phone as if about to call her.

                    JASIM
          Go ahead - and I can tell
          her about the man you let
          in the house today.

Husam swears under his breath. Thinks hard. Digs
into his pocket, pulls out some cash. Extends $20
to Jasim.

                    HUSAM
          Here, you can go to a movie
          or something before going
          home.

At this, Jasim becomes distrustful, suspicious.
He glances at the black backpack between Husam's
feet but takes the money as the bus slows to a
stop and fills with more passengers. Jasim sees
POLICE OFFICER #1 standing near the bus stop,
watching the passengers boarding and deboarding.
Despite Husam's expectation, followed by
insistent gestures, Jasim does not rise. Husam
can't make a scene without raising the attention
and suspicion of two passengers presently
watching him. The bus pulls away.

                    JASIM
          I just want to go downtown
          and look around a little. I
          want to see the Christmas
          tree.

Jasim studies Husam's pack again, looks around at
the new passengers, one of whom he exchanges
smiles with. He returns to watching the city
through the window. The buildings are getting
bigger, taller, the people dressed more
professionally. Husam seems increasingly anxious,
one knee bouncing.

                JASIM
       Where are you going anyway?

Husam doesn't answer but fishes in his pocket
again. Extends all he has left, another $60.
Jasim, surprised, is all the more suspicious.
Husam keeps his voice low so others won't hear,
as the bus is slowing to another stop.

                HUSAM
       Jasim, you can go downtown
       and spend all day and night
       there for all I care, but
       you have to get off the bus
       now and take the next bus
       in.

Jasim considers it, taking the money. He looks
around at the passengers. Looks at Husam's pack.

                JASIM
       Why?

                HUSAM
       I just don't want you
       around, all right? I'm
       meeting some friends....

Jasim doesn't buy it, but as the bus slows to a
stop, Husam practically lifts his brother out of

his seat by the sleeve of his jacket, moving him towards the aisle. Before Jasim can exit the row, Husam sees a uniformed policeman, POLICE OFFICER #2, boarding the bus. Husam pulls Jasim back down into his seat.

The officer works his way deliberately towards the back of the bus, scanning the passengers and their personal items. Husam, with his foot, quietly slides and nudges the black backpack over to between Jasim's feet, taking Jasim's pack and setting it on his own lap. He glances at his watch, sends a quick text, tucks the phone away as the officer approaches. Jasim pockets the money.

The officer stops next to the boys, profiling Husam particularly, studying him and the backpacks.

>POLICE OFFICER #2
>Where are you boys headed today? (to Jasim) Shouldn't you be in school?

>HUSAM
>I'm taking him downtown – to see the Christmas tree ... to do a little shopping, to buy a Christmas gift ... for our mother....

Jasim smiles, victorious. The officer isn't convinced.

                    HUSAM
          She's sick....

                    POLICE OFFICER #2
          What's in the packs?

Husam opens Jasim's pack. The officer peers in
and starts to reach in but waits until receiving
Husam's nodded permission to do so. He removes a
signed baseball, a boy's book about sailboats,
the tablet, a chart of sailor's knots, two
lengths of rope, a pudding cup, a lunch bag, a
Matchbox sports car. He looks from the toy car to
Husam, to Jasim, to the black backpack between
Jasim's feet.

                    POLICE OFFICER #2
                    (to Husam)
          You seem a little nervous
          today. (regards the lengths
          of rope and the knots
          chart) Do you know what a
          double sheet bend is?

Jasim reaches over, grabs the two lengths of
rope, ties a quick double sheet bend, extends it
to the officer proudly. The officer takes a call
on his radio, indicating with pointing his finger
for the black backpack to be opened as well – but
the dispatcher is requesting him elsewhere. After
a second lingering glance at the black backpack
and the boys, the officer smiles at Jasim, turns
and exits the bus to deal with the call. He waves
the bus on.

Husam checks the time, swears, sends a quick
text, begins reciting hadith softly in Arabic
beneath his breath.

My Kingdom

Jasim returns to looking through the window. The rising skyline now features skyscrapers, bustling pedestrians. The new passengers intrigue him, but he's distracted by the black backpack now between his own legs. As the bus slows at the next stop, Jasim rises on his own to exit, but Husam, seeing POLICE OFFICER #3 at the bus stop, makes Jasim stay seated. The bus is filling as it nears the heart of the city.

A YOUNG GIRL, Jasim's age, boards with her GRANDMOTHER. The girl is gorgeous, beautifully dressed in matching hat, gloves, sweater, skirt and warm tights. She's carrying a pair of ice skates. Jasim is captivated, smitten. The girl's grandmother is slow, uses a cane. The pair sit near the front in the handicap/elderly seats behind the driver, facing inwards. Jasim catches the girl's eye. They exchange smiles. She likes him too. The bus travels on.

Husam has noticed Jasim's interest in the girl.

>   HUSAM
> This is why women should be covered. You must strive, little brother, to be pious and pure of mind, to follow the will of Allah, to be a mujahid like our father was, to pursue jihad until death and nothing else.... You must promise me that you'll start attending mosque. If anything ever happens to me, you will have to become the man of the house.

                    JASIM
          Why would anything happen
          to you, Husam?

Husam doesn't answer. He checks the time, the bus route. They're approaching the heart of downtown. The skyscrapers tower above. The traffic is thick, the pedestrians thicker, the luxury storefronts bedecked with holiday decorations and displays. The bus is nearly full, some passengers standing. Jasim checks to ensure the girl is still aboard.

A man sitting across the aisle is watching the brothers. When his view is blocked by a standing passenger, Husam bends forward and pulls the black backpack towards him just enough to be able to open the zipper slightly, as casually as he can. Reaching into the pack, he turns something, a dial perhaps, double-checking his watch as he does so. Jasim catches a glimpse of looped electrical wires inside but glances away before Husam catches him looking. Husam closes and fastens the zipper-pulls together with a small lock.

Jasim, with growing worry, studies his brother, the preoccupied passengers, the innocent, busy pedestrians on the street. He looks around at the city, up at the skyline.

                    JASIM (quietly)
          I don't want to die today,
          Husam.

                    HUSAM
          You're not going to die.
          We're getting off at the
          next stop.

Jasim glances from the backpack to the girl - who
catches his eye and smiles again.

                    JASIM
          I don't want anyone else to
          die either.

                    HUSAM
          "To those who believe and
          do deeds of righteousness
          hath Allah promised
          forgiveness and a great
          reward."

                    JASIM
          What's in the backpack,
          Husam?

                    HUSAM
          Nothing you need to worry
          about.

Jasim looks out of the window.

                    JASIM
          I don't want to get off at
          the next stop.

Husam doesn't reply. Jasim glances at the girl,
her skates, the bus-route chart.

                    JASIM
          I want to get off at the
          ice-skating rink. It's only
          two more stops, I think.

Husam has been quietly, slowly with his foot,
pushing the black backpack under the seat ahead
of Jasim.

                    JASIM
          Father would have been
          brave enough to stay on the
          bus.

                    HUSAM
          I have not yet earned
          martyrdom. Today is but one
          battle in the long war.

                    JASIM
          Why must there be war,
          Husam? This place is so
          much better than where
          we're from. Everything is
          better here. Everyone lives
          better here. People are
          happier here. I'm happier
          here.

                    HUSAM
          We are not to live for
          happiness on earth, little
          brother, but to serve
          Allah, to sacrifice
          everything, our lives if
          asked, for Allah's rewards
          hereafter.

                        JASIM
            But I like the rewards
            here.

The bus is coming to a stop. Husam rises, returns
Jasim's backpack to him to carry. He pulls Jasim
along to follow him out. The black backpack has
been left hidden beneath the seat. Husam checks
to ensure Jasim is following him to the door.

EXT. BUS STOP - DAY

When Husam steps off the bus, he is distracted by
POLICE OFFICER #4 standing almost directly in
front of him, studying him intently. Husam
attempts to walk away nonchalantly. The bus door
hisses closed behind him. Husam turns to check on
Jasim — but Jasim has stayed on the bus and the
bus is pulling away. Husam can't make a scene
without drawing attention to himself.

As the bus travels another half block, a timer is
TICKING in Husam's head, growing louder. POLICE
OFFICER #4 is still watching him. The heavy metal
door of a freight-lift lid SLAMS shut nearby,
making Husam jump. The officer grows more
suspicious, seems ready to act.

In the middle of the block, the bus stops
suddenly. The bus doors open and the driver jumps
off, hurrying away without looking back. Other
passengers follow, hurriedly deboarding.

EXT. DOWNTOWN CHICAGO STREET - DAY

Husam swears, starts running towards the bus, ignoring the officer. A horn BLARES loudly near Husam, frightening him; he nearly falls over.

People are pouring off the bus, some running away, some helping others, passengers urging surrounding pedestrians to get back and stay back. Horns are HONKING as the traffic grinds to a halt. A driver behind the bus is urged to exit her vehicle.

Jasim and the girl help her grandmother off the bus through the bus's front door - they're the last off. Jasim sees Husam running towards them. When the grandmother is safely off, Jasim and the grateful girl exchange a quick glance. Jasim, gauging Husam's approach, leaps back on bus and sits in driver's seat. He figures out how to close the doors just as Husam arrives and begins banging on the door and yelling at Jasim to open it. The bus is still running. Sitting on the edge of the seat, Jasim figures out how to put the bus in gear.

The bus lurches forward and weaves ahead. A PASSENGER who had been sitting near the brothers grabs and grapples with Husam as the bus pulls away.

                    PASSENGER (incredulously)
        You left your brother on
        the bus...?

Husam struggles to free himself as an angry, accusing crowd gathers around him. Police officers are quickly approaching.

The bus careens through a red light without slowing. Car horns blare and braking tires screech as the bus clears the intersection. Husam tears free, leaving his jacket in the PASSENGER's hands. He starts chasing the bus on foot, the timer still ticking in his head, ever more loudly.

On the next block, the bus makes a hard turn, plowing over a street sign and into a tight one-way, open-ended service alley - where there are no pedestrians, no store windows, just high solid walls and solid doors on both sides.

INT. BUS IN ALLEY - DAY

Jasim drives halfway down the alley, where he stops the bus and turns off the engine, relieved. In the rearview mirror, he sees Husam turn the corner, hesitate a moment and start running towards him. Jasim opens the doors, steps off and starts towards Husam.

EXT. ALLEY - DAY

                    JASIM (motioning)
    Go back!

But Husam keeps running towards him, determinedly.

JASIM
                Stop! Husam, stop ...

To Jasim's dismay, Husam doesn't slow. Jasim
thinks, weighs, turns, jumps back on the bus.

INT. BUS - DAY

Jasim closes the bus doors again. He deliberates
half a moment and runs to the rear of bus,
grabbing his own backpack from off a front seat
along the way. He approaches the black backpack,
still under the seat. Jasim is unseen as Husam
reaches the side of bus and pounds on the rear
door, then tries to pry it open. Jasim rises and
runs to the front of the bus again. He opens the
doors - Husam leaps in the rear door.

                    JASIM
                Leave it, Husam! Come on!

Husam ignores him, goes to the black backpack and
attempts to retrieve it, praying all the while,
the timer in his head ticking ever more loudly.
But he can't extract the pack: Jasim has tied it
firmly to a seat leg with a length of his rope,
secured with one of his knots. Husam struggles
with the knot but can't figure out how to untie
it.

                    HUSAM
                Jasim!

But Jasim has vanished. Swearing, Husam runs
forward to the driver's seat and sits, ready to
drive the bus out of the alley and into the busy
street. But the key is not in the ignition. He

looks up. Jasim is standing some thirty feet ahead of the bus, facing it, his feet spread defiantly. Jasim raises the bus keys in his clenched hand. The timer in Husam's head stops ticking.

EXT. BUS - DAY

                    JASIM
        This is my city, Husam. My
        home. You will not harm it.

Husam, cursing, stands and retrieves a knife from his pocket. Opening the blade, he glances angrily at Jasim, then turns and runs towards rear of the bus. Camera on Jasim, watching, as the bus explodes.

Camera stays on Jasim as he turns away, raising his hands to protect his face, shards and pieces of glass and metal blowing by him, falling around him. He lowers his hands to glance at the destroyed bus, which remains off camera.

Car alarms blare and rising sirens wail as Jasim turns and walks away, slipping through the law enforcement line at the end of the alley.

EXT. DOWNTOWN CHICAGO - DAY

Jasim keeps walking, continuing into the heart of the shopping district. Within a few blocks, the activity is relatively normal again: busy shoppers, beautifully decorated windows. Sirens gradually fade. Holiday MUSIC is played by street MUSICIANS, sung by CAROLERS in front of a store.

Jasim stops to get a cup of hot cider and a
pretzel from a VENDOR, paying with the money his
brother gave him. The vendor notices that Jasim
is bleeding from a small cut on his cheek. Vendor
dabs at the cut with a napkin.

                    VENDOR
          You okay...?

                    JASIM (nods)
         Thanks ...

Vendor gives Jasim a clean napkin to hold on the
cut. On a TV in a nearby store window, there is
news coverage of the explosion. Jasim takes note
but he doesn't linger and moves on.

EXT. DALEY PLAZA - TWILIGHT

City lights are coming up. Offices are emptying
of workers hurrying home and to their holiday
shopping. Jasim gazes up in wonder as the
Christmas tree in Daley Plaza is lit.

EXT. ICE SKATING RINK, MILLENNIUM PARK - TWILIGHT

Coming around at last to the skating rink, Jasim
sees the girl's grandmother sitting rink side.
The girl is on the ice. She's a wonderful skater.
She sees him, smiles to him, circles to the
center of the ice and executes a graceful jump
and elegant spin, finishing in a thankful curtsy,
just for him.

Jasim goes to the skate rental counter.

                              ICE RINK EMPLOYEE
                    Size?

                              JASIM
                    Five, please.

The employee retrieves a pair of skates. Jasim
pays.

                              JASIM
                    Thank you.

                              ICE RINK EMPLOYEE
                    Ever skated before?

Jasim glances at the girl cutting long, smooth
curves around the rink.

                              JASIM
                    I'll figure it out.

On the bench, he finishes knotting the laces on
his skates, then rises and works his way out to
the center of the ice. From his POV, the camera
follows the girl skating around, then lifts,
rising, to follow the skyline up and into the
first of the evening stars above.

                                        FADE OUT:

                    THE END

QUENT CORDAIR

MY KINGDOM

"AT HOME WITH HEATHER JAMES"

A short screenplay

FADE IN:

INT. BAR - DAY

It's mid-afternoon as SAM (Samantha), an attractive, divorced, sharply dressed professional, hurries into an empty upscale bar, checking her watch. Upon seeing that CHARLIE, the bartender, is watching a soccer game on the TV behind the bar –

                SAM
     Charlie!

Charlie checks his watch.

              CHARLIE
     Sorry, Sam.

Charlie changes the TV to Channel 702. A laundry-detergent commercial is on. Sam lights a cigarette as Charlie mixes her usual. He retrieves an ashtray for her from its hiding place behind the "No Smoking" sign.

              CHARLIE (CONT'D)
     I thought you were getting
     tickets to this one.

                    SAM
          I tried. Are you kidding?
          There was already a line
          six blocks long at the
          studio this morning.

TV SHOW INTRO. - SERIES OF SHOTS

On the TV, the title "At Home with Heather James"
appears over an introductory series of shots
featuring HEATHER JAMES - learning a recipe from
a guest chef in the studio kitchen, practicing a
ballroom dance step in the studio living room,
demonstrating a pruning technique in the garden,
re-tiling a floor, attempting to teach her golden
retriever by example how to roll over, laughing
with a guest in the audience, learning decoupage
- always having a grand time. She's vivacious,
glowing, absorbed and focused; likes to ham it up
but can be serious too; interacts warmly and
easily with her audience, full of great zest for
life.

INT. TELEVISION STUDIO SET - DAY

The set is a cutaway of a well decorated,
comfortable home, kitchen on one side, living
room on the other. Above the fireplace is a large
flat-screen TV, presently displaying the show's
title. The live studio audience APPLAUDS.

                    ANNOUNCER (O.S.)
          Ladies and gentlemen -
          Heather James!

HEATHER JAMES walks onto the set, dressed more sexily than usual, judging by the OOHS, AHHS, a WOLF WHISTLE, surprised MURMERS and huge APPLAUSE from her audience. A little shy at the response to her outfit, Heather shows it off playfully and feigns surprise at their reaction.

                HEATHER
      What...?

Audience LAUGHS and APPLAUDS with an energetic, conspiratorial buzz.

                HEATHER (CONT'D)
      Well? What's a girl to do?

Audience LAUGHS.

                HEATHER (CONT'D)
      It's not as if anyone
      particularly special is
      coming by today....

Delight and even more enthusiasm in response. Heather puts on a Southern-belle drawl, playfully impetuous.

                HEATHER (CONT'D)
      Why, mother, I've never
      even met the man formally.
      I've only had the
      occasional glimpse of him
      from across the way, but
      you know how he affects me
      so. And you just had to
      invite him over for tea.

The audience LAUGHS, loving it. Heather drops the character.

> HEATHER (CONT'D)
> Today, we're back in the
> kitchen with my favorite
> chef, Tony Glenn, who's
> sharing a menu featuring
> lamb medallions with a
> black-olive wine sauce.
> (APPLAUSE) We'll check on
> the progress of our herb
> garden, which is coming in
> very nicely. (APPLAUSE)
> Artist Julie Morgan will
> continue our painting
> lesson. (APPLAUSE) But
> first, we have, ahem, a
> certain visitor....

Audience knows who it is, HOOTS and APPLAUDS wildly.

> HEATHER (CONT'D) (to
> camera)
> Don't go away.

APPLAUSE as the show cuts to commercial.

INT. BAR - DAY

> SAM
> Oh my god, the girl is
> going to melt right there
> in front of the whole
> world.

> CHARLIE
> You wouldn't?

                    SAM
          You know I keep my feet on
          the ground, sunshine.

BEAU BRALEY enters, spots the TV and checks his
watch. As he approaches the bar, Sam watches him
through the bar's mirror, sensing opportunity -

                    CHARLIE
          Uh, oh.

                    SAM
          Oh, shut up.

She hastily puts out the cigarette. Charlie slips
the ashtray behind the bar.

                    BEAU
          Would you mind if we turned
          it to Channel 702?

                    CHARLIE
          It's on.... What can I get
          for you?

                    BEAU
          Vodka rocks, thanks -
          olive.

Beau sits near Sam, leaving a barstool between
them. Sam checks him out on the sly. Beau is
dressed upscale casual. No wedding band. He's
attractive but more rugged than classically
handsome, and there's an intensity about him that
intrigues her.

> SAM
> So which is it — you're in love with Heather James, or you'd love to be Heather James?

Beau acknowledges her with a warmly polite smile but doesn't answer.

> SAM (CONT'D)
> Okay ...

"At Home with Heather James" is coming back on the TV.

INT. TELEVISION STUDIO SET - DAY

Heather is standing downstage-center. She shushes the APPLAUSE.

> HEATHER
> Thank you, thank you.... Of course our first guest needs no introduction on this show. For those of you watching for the first time, I only talk about him ... constantly – oh god, I'm losing it already. Without further ado, ladies and gentlemen, my favorite actor, Rex Keller.

My Kingdom

REX KELLER, an exceptionally handsome movie star, enters to uproarious APPLAUSE, a few hysteric SCREAMS. He appreciates the response warmly, sincerely, accustomed to it. He kisses Heather on both cheeks, causing her to go momentarily weak in the knees. She looks to the audience for support, and motions for Rex to sit with her in the "living room."

>   HEATHER (fanning herself)
>   Oh my. Dear me.

Rex smiles graciously.

>   HEATHER (CONT'D)
>   Well, Rex Keller. It's nice
>   to finally meet you.

>   REX
>   Likewise, Heather. I want
>   to thank you for your
>   generous compliments and
>   for keeping my name in
>   front of your audience –
>   for a while now, I
>   understand. I'm flattered.

Audience APPLAUDS madly.

>   HEATHER
>   Yes, you are – um –
>   appreciated here. Ahem,
>   anyway, my alleged excuse
>   for having you on the show
>   today is to talk about the
>   new movie you have coming
>   out in a few weeks –
>   Conner's Bronze?

                    REX
          Conner's Bronze. Yes, a
          departure from the action-
          adventure roles, but I was
          between projects and I
          thought I'd try this little
          independent film that
          happened to fall in my lap.
          Seemed like a good
          opportunity to stretch the
          wings, you know.

                  HEATHER
          What can you tell us about
          it, without giving too much
          away?

                    REX
          Sure, well, we do have a
          couple of clips, I believe?
          To set this first one up: I
          play Conner, an art
          collector, and an art
          gallery has sent me to one
          of their artists' studios
          to check out a recently
          completed sculpture.

                  HEATHER
          Sounds quite interesting
          already. Let's watch -

They both turn to the screen above the hearth.

My Kingdom

INT. SCULPTURE STUDIO - DAY

CONNER (played by Rex Keller) is walking slowly around an exquisite sculpture, a female nude bronze, half life-sized. The figure is a dancer, captured in a moment of joyful, expressive innocence and graceful ecstasy. Conner is utterly fascinated. Stopping in front of it, his hands are drawn to the figure, unconsciously following her curves, without touching. The setting is an in-home sculpture studio. He looks to SARA, the sculptor, who has paused from her work on a clay figure to watch him. She's taken with how affected he is. At his questioning glance, she nods her permission. He touches the piece, his fingers lightly traveling her lines, touching and tracing the hollows, the curves, the side of the face, her lips. Sara reacts with an intake of breath, feeling his touch as if on her own body.

INT. BAR - DAY

Beau is watching the film clip with a smile of quiet satisfaction. Sam studies his reaction with curiosity, her eyes traversing from Beau to the TV and back.

INT. SCULPTURE STUDIO - DAY

>   CONNER (enraptured)
>   Sara, she's magnificent....

Sara can't speak; she can only watch and feel, watching Conner intently, trying to make out who he might be, who he is, hoping that he's truly what he seems, but not yet certain or trusting.

                    CONNER (CONT'D)
          Yes, of course, she has to
          be mine.... I have to meet
          her....

                    SARA
          Meet - her?

                    CONNER
          The model. I have to meet
          her.

                    SARA
          The model?

                    CONNER
          She's what I want. She's
          all I want. This spirit.
          This soul. This way to live
          in the world. This
          innocent, bountiful,
          beautiful, guiltless joy.
          I've been searching for
          this, waiting for her - for
          all my life. I have to meet
          her.

                    SARA
          Yes, well, that might be
          arranged....

Conner continues to adore the sculpture. Sara
watches him, longing, wondering, doubting,
disappointed, torn, still feeling his hands as
they continue to touch.

MY KINGDOM

INT. TELEVISION STUDIO SET - DAY

Heather is silent, her eyes still on the screen after it has gone blank, remaining in the movie though it's no longer there. Her breath is quickened as she seems to be examining something within herself, as if someone had invaded a private place within her which she hadn't realized was there. Rex is waiting for her to say something, surprised that she's speechless. The audience, too, is silent, hanging on Heather's response.

INT. BAR - DAY

Beau watches Heather as if the future of his world depends on her reaction. Sam studies Beau via the mirror, tracing the rim of her glass with her finger.

INT. TELEVISION STUDIO SET - DAY

Heather remembers where she is. She blinks and looks at Rex, seeing him in an entirely new light. She gives no thought to the presence of her audience, speaking with Rex as if they were alone.

>   HEATHER
>   That's ... that's
>   wonderful, Rex. I mean, I
>   guess half the world knows
>   how ... how beautiful I
>   think you are. But that -
>   that - my god, Rex ... I
>   guess I never realized....

She searches his eyes, his face....

                    REX
          Thanks. I felt I was
          getting a bit pigeon-holed,
          you know. Thought I'd try
          my hand at a more serious,
          romantic role. It was a
          smaller film, but the story
          was pretty good, I thought.
          It was fun. A nice change.

                    HEATHER
          Fun? A nice change? Rex,
          this is phenomenal.
          Admittedly, I've been a
          walking billboard for you
          for years now - but, Rex,
          this ... this is serious,
          seriously good. This gets
          me....

A prompter off-screen manages to flag Heather's
attention.

                    HEATHER (CONT'D)
          Oh. Oh, yes, I guess we're
          going ... going to a
          commercial....

Someone starts to CLAP in the audience; another
joins in; the CLAPPING rises to APPLAUSE. Heather
doesn't hear them. Her gaze has returned to his
face, his eyes, his lips - as the show cuts to
commercial.

INT. BAR - DAY

                    SAM
          Jesus Christ, she's got it
          bad.

Beau has allowed himself a small smile of satisfaction.

>   SAM (CONT'D)
>   You're a deep one.

Beau takes note of her. She's intelligent and very attractive.

>   SAM (CONT'D)
>   So, what is it that you
>   like so much about our Ms.
>   Heather?
>
>   BEAU (as much to himself)
>   She's always in love, even
>   when she's not.

Sam waits for the explanation.

>   BEAU (CONT'D)
>   Even when she hasn't yet
>   found what she's looking
>   for, she's in love with the
>   thought of it. She's in
>   love with love, in love
>   with life, with the whole
>   of her life and everything
>   in it. Such a joy to watch.
>
>   SAM
>   You've been watching her
>   for a while then?
>
>   BEAU
>   Three years. Nearly every
>   day.

							SAM
					Well, apparently she
					imagines she's found her
					Mr. Wonderful. Rather
					naïve, don't you think?

							BEAU
					Rex? She'll figure him out.
					Heather James can't afford
					to be naïve.

							SAM
					Ah, Rex will have his
					customary fling with her.
					She'll be in heaven for a
					few whirlwind weeks or
					months, then she'll get her
					heart broken and be all the
					closer to learning –
					learning that it's better
					to have someone to come
					home to.

Beau hears a hopeful suggestion in that last, but
he doesn't answer. Sam backs off for the moment.

							SAM (CONT'D)
					Still water.... I'm Sam, by
					the way.

							BEAU
					Beau, Beau Braley.

							SAM
					Pretty name. Sounds
					familiar... You're not an
					actor....

                    BEAU
          No.

                    SAM
          But - you worked on that
          film?

He appreciates her perceptiveness but doesn't
answer directly. She checks her look in the
mirror.

                    SAM (CONT'D)
               (rising)
          Excuse me.

With her purse, she goes to the ladies' room as
the show is coming on again.

INT. TELEVISION STUDIO SET - DAY

The APPLAUSE dies down. Heather still isn't
acknowledging the audience; she's still absorbed
in Rex, who is increasingly uncomfortable with
her sudden intensity and attention. But he's
beginning to sense an opportunity.

                    HEATHER
          Wow.

                    REX
          Wow. I'm glad you like it.

                    HEATHER
          Oh, somehow "like" doesn't
          cut it.

                    REX
Well, I have to give credit
to the writing and the
directing, you know, which
were just superb, and the
other talent who gave me so
much to work with and -

          HEATHER (interrupting)
So, tell me, Rex Keller,
what's your favorite work
of art?

                    REX
I, um, well, that was a
nice sculpture we were
working with in the film. I
can't recall the name of
it. But I guess I like lots
of different kinds of -
Why? What kind of art do
you like?

                    HEATHER
I like that movie of yours,
and if that isn't great
art, I don't know what is.
So romantic, Rex. So
passionate. It's so - me.
Your character, Conner, was
saying things that I
thought only I ... And the
sculptor, Sara - it was
almost as if I were ... as
if you were ... oh god -
how did you do that?

                        REX (laughs)
            Usually, I don't know how I
            do it: I just - do it. It's
            just pretend, you know.
            There are a few tricks of
            the trade when it's not
            coming easily but -

                        HEATHER
            No, stop being modest. It
            doesn't become you. That
            couldn't have been
            pretending. I mean, not
            really. You meant it, in a
            way, didn't you? I mean, to
            do that, to play someone so
            deeply passionate - to be
            that, you have to draw on
            something inside, don't
            you? Maybe a deeper part
            that you don't necessarily
            show the public? A part we
            haven't seen before?

                        REX (going with it)
            I'm a romantic guy, I
            think.

He looks to the audience who APPLAUDS
supportively.

                        HEATHER
            The part about looking and
            waiting for someone ... for
            just the right, ideal
            someone....

                    REX
          I haven't settled down yet,
          have I?

                    HEATHER
          Surely you wouldn't be
          "settling" ... You must be
          waiting for someone as
          wonderful and passionate
          and beautiful as you
          are....

                    REX
          Oh, stop it already! You're
          too much. Adorably too
          much. Would you like to see
          the second clip?

                    HEATHER
          Mm-hmm....

Audience APPLAUDS enthusiastically, loving it.

INT. BAR - DAY

Sam, returning from the ladies' room, catches her
reflection in the mirror, makes a quick
adjustment to her hair, checks her freshened
lipstick. Beau doesn't acknowledge her return;
he's watching the screen intently. She finally
catches his eye; smiles as disarmingly as she's
able. Charlie, while replacing her drink, gives
her a teasing look of warning. She glares at him.
Determined, she takes a chance and sits on the
barstool next to Beau. Being polite, and focused
on the show, he doesn't protest. Charlie slides
her drink over. This close, she has enough
comportment not to turn and look at him directly,
but she can still see his face in the mirror.

INT. TELEVISION STUDIO SET - DAY

Rex and Heather are turning to watch the TV screen.

                    REX
          Let's see, in this one, the
          model for the sculpture,
          Madeleine - she's a dancer
          - she and I have met and
          we've been in a
          relationship for a while.
          We're at my place, I
          believe.

INT. CONNER'S LIVING ROOM - NIGHT

Conner enters his home. MUSIC is playing, a classical piece with an edge of melancholic frustration. Firelight and candlelight reveal the beautiful, classically trained dancer, MADELEINE, dancing, her attention focused on the same sculpture that was in the studio, now featured prominently in Conner's living room on a pedestal. Her dance advances toward the sculpture, slips away, then approaches from another angle as she watches the sculpture, sizing it up, eyeing the figure as if it were a competitor. She doesn't yet see Conner.

As the music rises to a paused, held climax, Madeleine brings her dance to a climactic pose, an attempted duplication of the pose of the sculpture. She seems to accomplish it physically, but somehow the spirit is different: the pose of the sculpture is light, natural, a moment of captured motion, of easy joy; Madeleine's pose is static, strained, forced.

She sees Conner watching her. Conner's gaze goes from Madeleine to the sculpture, where his gaze remains. Disappointed, Madeleine continues with her dance as the music continues. She re-approaches the sculpture and strikes the pose again, looking to Conner hopefully, defiantly, for his response, which he tries to mask, unsuccessfully. She has failed again.

Angrily she spins, her arm hitting and toppling the sculpture to the floor. Her eyes flash to Conner for his reaction. Reflexively, he had started toward the piece to save it, but he couldn't possibly reach it in time. His eyes close, afraid of what he will see. The CRASHING sound of the bronze hitting the floor isn't good. He looks to see that the arm of the sculpture has broken off. Madeleine has cut her own arm, but Conner goes first to the sculpture.

> MADELEINE
> It's a stupid piece of bronze, Conner. Look at it, it's hollow. I'm here, I'm real – warm flesh and blood – with a beating heart inside – a heart that loves you.... I'll have it repaired, I promise, as good as new.... I'm a good person, Conner. You always tell me how beautiful I am. I don't know what else you want me to be. That may be my body, but I don't ... I don't know who she is. She's not me. I'm not her.... What do you want, Conner? Tell me what you want. Do you know?

Conner goes to the broken sculpture. He kneels, picks it up and cradles it in his arms. He takes the arm and tenderly attempts to put it back in place.

                   MADELEINE
                   (CONT'D)
    Conner?

Conner looks to Madeleine and again to the sculpture, torn.

                 MADELEINE (CONT'D)
        You'll go to your grave
        with nothing but a cold
        piece of metal lying next
        to you....

Conner's eyes lift from the sculpture to appraise the whole of Madeleine's person. His expression shifts to pained apology. Madeleine turns and walks out. As Conner watches the door through which she's gone, his hand unconsciously caresses the wounded sculpture, as if to ease its pain.

INT. TELEVISION STUDIO SET - DAY

Heather is transfixed again, nearly drunk with emotion.

                 HEATHER
    Rex, what happens?

                   REX (laughs rather
                      nervously)
    Come on! You know I can't
    tell you that.

                    HEATHER
          No, I have to know, Rex. I
          need to know what happens.
          This is important.

                    REX
          Just a couple of weeks and
          the whole world will know.

                    HEATHER
          Would you have stayed with
          her? What's he going to do?

                    REX
          What Conner would do and
          what I might do isn't
          necessarily the same thing,
          you know: I'm an actor.
          Conner's a character. It's
          a story.

But he's been regarding Heather with growing
interest.

                    REX (CONT'D)
          A guy might be crazy to let
          a girl as sincere, loving
          and beautiful as Madeleine
          go....

                    HEATHER (unsure)
          Yeah, crazy.... What more
          could a man want...? She'd
          always love him, would
          always be there for him.
          And it's only a
          sculpture....

> REX
> You know – in art, in movies and books, we have the liberty of indulging in a little escapism, throwing it all to the wind, pursuing a romantic ideal....

> HEATHER
> And in real life?

> REX
> In real life – in real life, you're as enchanting in person as everyone told me you would be. And I hear you're a decent cook.

APPLAUSE and LAUGHTER as the obvious understatement breaks the tension. Heather ignores the audience, trying to read beneath Rex's exterior, hoping and trusting that there's so much more to him.

> HEATHER
> I can cook. What's your favorite dish?

> REX
> Um, I don't know. Do you have favorites of everything?

> HEATHER
> Why, Yes. Yes, I do. I'm kind of – known for that.

Audience LAUGHS and APPLAUDS in acknowledgment.

                    HEATHER (CONT'D)
          What is it that you really
          want, Rex Keller, want so
          badly you'd move heaven and
          earth to get...? You'd
          search for it, wait for it,
          for years and years if you
          had to, endure nights of
          loneliness and - (glancing
          at the blank screen) I want
          to know the ending, Rex.

                    REX
          If you'll have dinner with
          me tonight, I'll invite you
          to go with me to the red-
          carpet premiere of the film
          next weekend. You'll see
          the ending as soon as
          humanly possible.

Audience GASPS in surprise and hovers on the edge
of expectation.

                    HEATHER
          You don't have ... a video
          copy of it or something? I
          have to wait until next
          weekend?

Rex shakes his head with a half-astonished laugh;
the audience MURMURS, echoing his response.

                    HEATHER (CONT'D)
          You could tell me the
          ending then, privately?

                    REX
          Fact is, I don't even know
          the ending myself. We shot
          a lot of stuff at the end,
          and I'm not entirely sure
          how it was all edited and
          pieced together.

                    HEATHER
          Oh. But it has to have a
          good ending....

                    REX
          I would be honored to pick
          you up at eight?

                    HEATHER
          This evening? Oh - dinner
          ... I've made this all
          rather convenient for you,
          haven't I...? And you'll
          take me to see the
          premiere....

Rex nods.

                    HEATHER (CONT'D)
          Well, yes then. Thank you.

Uproarious APPLAUSE.

INT. BAR - DAY

Beau has seen all he needs to see. As he finishes his drink and motions for the bill, Sam lets her napkin slip to the floor between them. She steadies herself on him as she retrieves it, leaving her hand on his arm for a moment longer than necessary.

INT. TELEVISION STUDIO SET - DAY

                    HEATHER
          I can't wait to see this
          film. Beautiful work, Rex.
          So romantic.

                    REX
          I'll see you this evening
          then?

Heather nods and they stand; he kisses her on the
cheek for longer than necessary, making her
blush.

                    HEATHER
          Ladies and gentlemen, Rex
          Keller. See him soon in a
          theatre near you, in
          Conner's Bronze.

Rex exits to APPLAUSE.

                    HEATHER (CONT'D)
          Well! Goodness. I'm the dog
          who's caught the car. Now
          what do I do? Is he the
          real thing?

By their reaction, the audience seems to think
so. Heather is hopeful, but not entirely sure.
Her off-screen prompter brings her back into the
moment.

                    HEATHER
          Oh, yes - stay with us.
          Next up - chef Tony Glenn.

INT. BAR - DAY

As the tab comes, Beau reaches for his wallet.

                    SAM
          Have another drink with me.

Beau lays two bills on the bar; indicates he's paying for both his and hers.

                    BEAU
          Thanks, but (glancing at
          the screen) there's someone
          I have to meet.

He gives Sam a polite nod and a smile as he turns and exits. Through the mirror Sam watches him go. Once he's through the door, she turns to stare after him. Charlie replaces her empty glass with another drink, which she reaches for without looking. She looks from the door, to the TV, to the door again, wondering.

                    SAM
          You don't think...?

                    CHARLIE
          Nah.

Still regarding the door, she reaches for another cigarette.

                    SAM
          Damn.

As she turns back to the bar, Charlie already has the cigarette lighter lit and waiting.

                    CHARLIE
          A blind fool, honey. A
          blind fool.

INT. TELEVISION STUDIO CONTROL ROOM - NIGHT

Heather is alone in the control room except for
her ASSISTANT sitting nearby, finishing up some
work. It's the end of the day; the lights are
being switched off. The Assistant waves to an
employee who's leaving for the night. The studio
is relatively quiet. Heather is absorbed in the
Conner's Bronze clips, which she's replaying on a
monitor, the sound low. She rewinds to the first
clip, in which Conner is caressing the sculpture.
The Assistant observes Heather studying.

                    HEATHER
          It feels so oddly familiar.

The Assistant turns to watch the clip with her.

                    ASSISTANT
          If you were a man, that
          would be you, Heather. The
          way he touches things, the
          way he loves what he loves,
          wants what he wants....

Heather's fingers unconsciously rise to touch and
caress Conner's image on the screen.

                    ASSISTANT (CONT'D)
          I think you've got Rex
          Keller.

                    HEATHER
          I want Conner....

SECURITY GUARD (O.S. over
                    intercom)
          Ms. James?

                    HEATHER
          Yes?

                    SECURITY GUARD
                    (O.S.)
          There's a Mr. Beau Braley
          here to see you?

                    HEATHER
          I don't know a Beau Br- ...
          wait.

Heather rewinds the provided footage, scanning
accompanying info. The name sounds familiar to
the Assistant as well, who checks her notes.

                    HEATHER (CONT'D)
          Copyright, Beau Braley.

                    ASSISTANT
          I think he's the producer.

                    HEATHER (on intercom to
                    SECURITY GUARD)
          Show him in.

SECURITY GUARD accompanies Beau to the door.
Heather checks him over. He seems okay. And
somehow more than okay. She nods to the guard,
who exits. Beau glances at the Assistant; Heather
realizes Beau would prefer privacy; she
hesitates, but looks to the Assistant who
understands and rises to go. Heather restarts the
clips from the beginning; they begin playing on
the monitor, the sound low.

> ASSISTANT
> Have a great time tonight.
> You deserve the best.

> HEATHER
> Thanks. Goodnight.

After the Assistant leaves –

> HEATHER
> This is your film?

> BEAU
> Yes.

There's an attraction between them which she doesn't understand, catching her off-guard. His intensity and interest in her are unmistakable.

> HEATHER
> You were watching today?

> BEAU
> I was.

> HEATHER
> Then you know I have a date tonight. I should be going.

> BEAU
> No, you're going with me tonight –

From his jacket pocket he produces a small film canister.

> BEAU (CONT'D)
> – to see a movie.

                    HEATHER
          That's Conner's Bronze?

Beau opens the canister and hands her a length of
cut film strip. She uncurls it, holding it up to
the light, looking at the individual frames.

                    HEATHER (CONT'D)
          You would show me the rest
          of it?

                    BEAU
          All of it.

                    HEATHER
          The ending?

                    BEAU
          The beginning, the ending,
          and every breath between.

Heather examines the film strip again, her eyes
falling on a frame with Rex in close-up.

                    HEATHER
          Does he know you're here?

Beau shakes his head.

                    HEATHER (CONT'D)
          And why do you think I'll
          go with you?

                    BEAU
          Because you're Heather
          James.

She searches his eyes defiantly. She doesn't know whether to slap him or kiss him or call security. She knows that he knows that he's hooked her. She looks at the film - and pushes the intercom button on the console.

>   SECRETARY (O.S.)
>   Yes, Ms. James?
>
>   HEATHER
>   Call Mr. Keller.
>
>   SECRETARY (O.S.)
>   Rex Keller, ma'am?
>
>   HEATHER
>   The number is on my desk.
>   Ask him if I can take a
>   rain check. Someone -
>   something has come up.
>
>   SECRETARY (O.S.)
>   But, Ms. James -
>
>   HEATHER
>   Just do it, please.
>
>   SECRETARY (O.S.)
>   Yes, Ms. James.

Heather gathers her things.

>   HEATHER
>   This had better be good.

Beau holds the door for her.

MY KINGDOM

INT. BEAU'S LIVING ROOM - NIGHT

Heather is watching Conner's Bronze on the big screen in Beau's living room, shown from a film projector. She's curled cozily on the sofa, wrapped in a throw, shoes off, legs tucked beneath her, totally absorbed in the film. Beau watches her from the entry to the dining area. Her expression shifts with each shift of emotion on the screen. She's hanging on each word, living and dying with the characters. Beau is wholly taken with her.

He turns to the dining area quietly. He's wearing an apron. He lights the candles on the romantically set table and slips back into the kitchen to check his cooking. Heather takes no notice of him as she continues watching. On the screen is playing the very end of the scene in which Conner is considering his broken sculpture, his finger tracing the jagged edge tenderly. The scene fades to:

INT. SCULPTURE STUDIO - DAY

Conner enters through the ajar door to Sara's studio. MUSIC can be heard. Sara is not in the room, but Sara's young female APPRENTICE pauses from her sweeping as Conner locates his repaired sculpture and approaches it.

                    APPRENTICE
        She's yours?

Conner nods, looking closely for evidence of the repair.

                    APPRENTICE (CONT'D)
          All better. Not even a
          scar.

                    CONNER
          Remarkable.

He looks around for Sara. The Apprentice nods in
the direction of an open door, which leads out
onto a small back lawn surrounded by a garden.
Conner moves in that direction.

EXT. SARA'S LAWN AND GARDEN - CONTINUOUS

The MUSIC is coming from a phone, Bluetooth
speaker. Sara is dancing, barefoot in the grass,
laughing as her dog frolics with her, trying to
join in. The music gradually rises to a paused
climax, at which Sara's dance peaks - in the
exact pose of the sculpture, with all the
sculpture's spirit and joy. She sees Conner
watching. Surprised and happy to see him, she
smiles her beautiful smile. As the music
continues, she spins on.

Conner begins to understand, to realize. He takes
off his shoes and socks, and walks out to her. He
takes her hand in his, his other hand goes to her
waist, and he moves her into a dance. The
Apprentice watches from the door.
While the music continues, they slow to a stop,
until they're standing still before each other,
arms and hands falling to their sides as they
watch each other's eyes. Sara's hands rise,
following, tracing but not quite touching, the
curve of his abdomen, his chest, his shoulders.
But then she can't move her hands anymore: her
wrists are in his grasp. He pulls her into him
and kisses her. The world spins about them as the

music rises. The Apprentice smiles, slips back into studio, giving them privacy.

INT. SCULPTURE STUDIO - CONTINUOUS

The Apprentice returns to her sweeping, humming to the music, dancing with the broom. She gives the sculpture a passing, loving caress. Camera tracks around the sculpture. The Conner's Bronze credits begin to roll.

INT. BEAU'S LIVING ROOM - NIGHT

Heather watches as "Produced by Beau Braley" scrolls, her expression intense, nearly unreadable.

Upon seeing "Directed by Beau Braley," an eyebrow lifts. After "Written by Beau Braley" has scrolled, she could be scooped off the sofa with a spoon.

Heather's eyes leave the screen. She manages to collect herself, and she turns to look at Beau in a new light. His apron in hand, he's leaning against the archway between the living room and the dining room, watching her. They regard each other for an extended moment. Beau checks the screen, watching for something. He nods for Heather to look at the screen again. A space opens at the end of the credits, into which the text scrolls and holds: "For my favorite - " Heather begins to smile in disbelief. Beau approaches and stands in front of her. She looks up at him. He takes her hand and raises her to her feet.

                    HEATHER
            For your - favorite?

                     BEAU
            For my favorite flower....

Heather knows what's coming, and there's nothing
she can do about it. And she thinks she likes it.
Really likes it. Beau's hands are rising, not yet
touching, only a breath's distance from her body,
following the curve of her torso, her shoulders,
her cheek, her lips....

                    HEATHER
            Your favorite - flower?

His mouth is very near hers.

                    HEATHER (CONT'D)
            What's your favorite
            flower, Beau Braley?

His fingers are in her hair, behind her neck....

                     BEAU
            Heather, of course.

                    HEATHER
            Good answer.

He pulls her into his kiss. She melts.

INT. BEAU'S BEDROOM - DAY

The morning after. The doors to the terrace are
open, curtains touched by the breeze. In a white
terry robe, Beau sits not far from the bed,
typing intently in a notebook computer, cup of
coffee nearby. He has a fine view of the vista

outside, and a fine view of Heather in his bed. She is just now waking. Her head still on the pillow, she watches Beau lovingly.

> HEATHER
> Poor Rex.

> BEAU
> Rex was well paid for his services.

> HEATHER
> Is that a new script?

Beau nods while continuing to work.

> HEATHER
> Have you finished it yet?

Beau shakes his head.

> HEATHER (CONT'D)
> Can I read it?

> BEAU
> When I'm finished.

> HEATHER (after a pause)
> Finished yet?

Beau shoots her a playful glare.

> HEATHER (CONT'D)
> I love your stories, Beau Braley, especially the endings.... (to herself, with extra meaning) Oh, the endings....

Her eyes fall on a sculpture in the bedroom, the very sculpture featured in Conner's Bronze. She smiles, her head still on the pillow. Beneath the sheets, her body stretches and arches contentedly into the shape of the sculpture's pose; outside the sheets, her arm, fingers, foot and toes finish the pose naturally, perfectly, as her eyes close and she drifts again towards a peaceful sleep. Beau has been watching her. He smiles like a man who owns the world, and half the stars too. Returns to his writing.

FADE OUT:

THE END

My Kingdom

QUENT CORDAIR

Selections from Idolatry

A novel in five parts

by Quent Cordair

QUENT CORDAIR

My Kingdom

The Fountain

From Genesis, Part I of Idolatry

It was hardly the largest or most ornate fountain she had ever seen, and she had seen many in her travels, yet the more closely she approached, the more captivated she became. Its lower tier was composed of four remarkably lifelike elephants, facing the four winds, water spouting from their trunks, each creature captured in its own motion and mood. The southerly elephant was stomping in agitation, trunk cocked high and to the side. The easterly animal was bracing defiantly, head lowered and ears back, trunk pointing outwards. She circled to the northerly creature, who bore its burden with resignation, its trunk swinging low. The westerly elephant was the youngest of the four; it seemed eager to trot away at the first excuse, ears perked and flapping happily. She thought the elephants magnificent. She wanted to name them all and feed them and ride the youngest to the sea, where they would sit together in the sand and eat pistachios and watch the waves for hours on end.

The elephants were positioned between four columns, each of which was exotically adorned with bundles of reeds, Egyptian motifs, and capitals of palm fronds. A herd of small antelope peered out from around the columns. Some nibbled on the reeds; others drank from the fountain's pool. The elephants and columns supported a wide, spouted bowl, around the rim of which lounged the figures of three graceful girls of about Sira's age: one lay prone, her chin resting on her clasped hands as she admired her own reflection in the water below; another was supine, her leg bent and raised at the knee, her arm hanging loosely off the side of the bowl's rim, her face to the sun; the third was sitting with her knees drawn to her chest as she contemplated the fountain's central figure, which stood majestically on a stepped circular dais rising out of the upper pool.

The rendering of the elephants, the antelope, and the three girls was so masterful as to be nearly beyond Sira's ability to grasp or accept. Surely these living, breathing beings had been turned to stone in an instant by the Gorgons and they would spring to life again the moment the spell was broken. But when her gaze had risen to the top tier, she felt as if she herself might have come under the Gorgons' spell: her feet were rooted to the spot where she stood. She couldn't take her eyes off of the figure of the woman above.

At any moment, the woman's name or title would spring to mind. Sira was certain she recognized her—yet, she couldn't remember. . . . She was a great queen, or the wife of a dignitary Sira had met, or a distant relative, or a friend of her mother's—but no, perhaps this was a goddess of whom Sira had not yet heard. . . .

The stone of the fountain was unblemished, practically new by all appearances, barely weathered—which struck Sira as strange: she realized she had never before seen freshly carved, new sculpture in the round. Apparently, it just wasn't being done anymore. She thought to ask her father why this was so, why the only other such sculptures she had seen, save for the occasional frieze on a government building or mausoleum, was weather-beaten, crumbling or partially destroyed, why it was that the beautiful fountains and statues were always old, deteriorating and historical—relics of the past—and how it could be so, when this could be done? The fountain was perfect and gorgeous and young and uplifting, as fresh and bright as the dawn after a rain-washed night.

Scattered about its lower rim were offerings of flowers and fruit, but there was no clue to the figure's identity, no identifying prop or symbol. The woman was dressed simply but elegantly in the classic tunica, stola and palla. An exposed swath of the tunica, from the shoulder to the waist, was so sheer and revealing that the woman may as well have been partially nude—the nipple of her right breast and her navel were clearly visible beneath the transparent stone fabric. Flanking the figure, on the steps below, were the figures of two young boys, one sitting, the other kneeling, each holding a tilted amphora from which water flowed and converged to cascade down the steps and into the pool below. The woman wasn't tall, yet she seemed to stand taller, and more comfortably so, than any sculpted figure Sira had ever seen. Her chin was lifted slightly, arms held loosely to her sides, hands relaxed. She was regal yet approachable, worldly wise yet light of spirit, nothing more and nothing less than a woman standing in the place where she stood, the whole of the earth as her kingdom and home. Sira found her enchantingly beautiful, shiningly intelligent, passionately feminine, faultlessly virtuous—all that a girl could want to see, all that a girl could want to be.

For Sira, it was turning out to be a most extraordinary and wondrous day, and in such a remote, nondescript town, no less. When her family had entered the town's gate, the place had promised nothing beyond the ordinary, and now she felt as if she were falling deeply in love for the second time within the hour, first with the boy, and now with this woman. . . .

The Dance

From A New Eden, Part II of Idolatry

He turned and walked away. When he was halfway to the door he paused and cut left, through the tables. He stopped in front of the jukebox, dropped two coins in, pressed three buttons and turned back to face her. There was just enough space between the tables. He held out his hand.

She went to him.

Any eyes that hadn't followed them before were on them now. There was no way his fiancée wouldn't hear about it. Out of the corner of Paige's eye, she saw one of the girls slip her hand into her purse for her phone. Ian was going to pay for this, surely, and dearly—and she loved him for it.

When she came to him, his left hand took her right, and his right hand went to the small of her back. As he moved her in a slow circle to the country waltz, she closed her eyes, willing herself to let go.

Would that you could be
Mine then we would be
All that two should be,
Dancing in time. . . .

He had drawn her close, and it was all she could do to keep from leaning in and letting her cheek rest against his cheek, from letting her lips brush his neck, to taste the leather and prairie grass after a thunderstorm. . . .

Though close, I miss you,
Long so to kiss you,
It would be bliss to
Write our own rhyme. . . .

My Kingdom

The world had gone away and she didn't want it back—

But she threw a cold steel girder across the abyss to arrest the fall of her tumbling heart. Her heart hit it hard, and it hurt, but she couldn't get involved. Not here. Not with Ian. Not with anybody. She couldn't have complications. She couldn't be in anyone's hold and sway. Her life depended on staying unencumbered, on remaining neutral, agile, flexible, free. Unencumbered she could do, and do well, but not the other. Not this. She knew how to fly, but only without a harness or net. With safety she would become careless, her focus slipping, her attention wandering—she would sleep too soundly, her awareness softening, reflexes slowing. She would make a mistake, and a single mistake could kill her, could send her crashing and burning down through any net no matter how strong. It was safer to fly when falling wasn't an option.

It was just as well that Ian was engaged. It was damned fortunate, really.

She knew he had felt her bracing, stiffening as the song came to its inevitable end. After the last note played, there was silence in the room. Everyone was watching them, she knew. She didn't care.

He searched her eyes, looking for an answer.

There was none there to be found. Letting go of her hands, he took a step back and nodded politely.

"Thank you for the dance, Miss Keller."

"Thank you for asking, Mr. Argent."

He lingered a moment more before turning and walking away in his unhurried cowboy's gait. He let the door swing closed behind him without looking back.

She stood watching the door, asking herself what she had done, what she hadn't done, before returning to the bar, ignoring the eyes of all.

"Sandal, I think I'll have tequila."

QUENT CORDAIR

The Child

From The Fruit of the Tree (working title)
Part III of Idolatry (work in progress)

The lines had shuffled forward. Paige found herself standing next to the mother. The baby, bundled in her arms, had settled and calmed. He was so beautiful, so right, his blue eyes as clear and complete as little planets, encircled with rays of long blond lashes. His lips were ripe petals, formed for ready suckling. His ivory skin was of the most translucent, softest white marble imaginable, a glowing blush in the cheeks only the most accomplished painter might capture. Every little hillock and vale of his little body's topography, every rise and fall, every curve and round—it was all mere suggestion of the man to come, all mere promise, and yet, here he was, already present, already real. And *flawless*. To mothers everywhere, in all times, all but the most unfortunate babies are perfection, but Paige simply couldn't imagine any woman wanting anything more or less than what this woman held in her arms—a complete little world in himself, needing and wanting nothing more, lacking nothing, being everything. There was nothing to add, nothing to subtract, nothing to change. *This*—this perfect little thing should be untouchable, undefilable, always and forever. How could anything on earth or in heaven be more perfect and whole, in and unto itself? If only it could remain so, if only he might never come to know a moment of sorrow, of pain, of evil, of disappointment. Paige wanted to draw a circle of protection around him, an impenetrable halo of sacredness, to suspend time.

She was blinking away a welling wetness in her eyes. An ache had come to her heart, her stomach: she herself would never have that. She would never have what this woman had. She had never really even wanted it until now, never wanted a child, but at this moment, she found herself wanting it more than anything in the world. How could any woman not?

My Kingdom

    She looked up to find the mother watching her, with eyes that understood. Woman to woman, the one knew the other's ache, recognizing the depth of the longing in a woman-child who had lost her own mother, a daughter who wanted nothing more in that moment than to be a mother herself.

    The mother glanced down at her child and back up to Paige. Wordlessly, she asked the question.

    Paige could only nod, blinking back tears, stunned at the kindness of the offering, a place inside her heart breaking open.

    As she accepted the baby, her arms naturally, gently formed around him. It felt so right. She felt her entire body, her entire soul, warm with joy. He was so small, so light. She gazed into the blue orbs, perfect worlds of their own, as they gazed back into hers. She marveled at the beauty of the little face in all its wondrous glory. He was staring back into her face, a face new to him, seemingly as fascinated with her as she was with him. Her rocking sway, a gentle bounce, had started without her realizing or intending it. She began humming a melody. Her lullaby. Skye's lullaby . . .

QUENT CORDAIR

Author Q & A

An interview with Sadye Scott-Hainchek
Staff Writer for
The Fussy Librarian

Author and artist Quent Cordair has come a long, long way from his upbringing.

He was raised, in his words, in an "insular fundamentalist religious sect," but the local library gave him a critical window into the outside world.

Like many writers, he spent time in a variety of unrelated jobs to support his creative work, and the wait has paid off.

A fan of Cordair's recommended that we interview the acclaimed author of several short-story collections, novels, and screenplays, who also runs an art gallery in Napa with his wife.

SADYE: In your own words, you were "raised in an insular, fundamentalist religious sect." What effect do you think this has had on your writing?

QUENT: I was born and raised Pentecostal, a fundamentalist denomination of evangelical, charismatic Protestantism. It took me years as a young adult to work my way out of the sect, then progressively out of Christianity, out of religion, and finally out of mysticism altogether.

The legacy of my upbringing, yes, is stamped on my mind and soul, indelibly. It's always with me, as an unforgettable, inescapable part of my history.

For better and worse, I have the intimate experience and knowledge of that deeply religious way of thinking and of viewing the world, of believing Man to be incurably flawed and base in nature, of holding faith to be superior to reason, of viewing life on Earth as a journey merely to be endured, a time of struggle against physical desires and worldly wants in exchange for eternal reward in the hereafter.

That orientation to life and the world is nearly the opposite of what I've come to believe and practice today. ...

All I've experienced and learned on my journey, from that to this, very much influences my writing, especially my current work in progress.

The *Idolatry* story, a five-part novel series, revolves around how we view ourselves as a species — our deepest judgment of who we are as humans, of our place in the universe —and how our deepest premises about our identity and nature affect our personal relationships, our politics, our philosophy, the art we create, and especially — our love lives.

SADYE: You're a visual artist and a verbal artist — how do these two talents affect each other?

QUENT: For me, they're complementary, fascinatingly so. I can set painting aside, even for years on end, trading brush for pen, and find myself noticeably a better painter on return to the easel. I can return

My Kingdom

to writing from having painted solely for long stretches to find myself a better writer.

While the media and tools of the arts may be different, the art of the art, the esthetic principles and practice, are fundamentally the same.

When I write, it's often as though I'm trying to paint with words. When I paint, I'm trying to tell a story with line and color.

SADYE: Have you done all of your book covers?

QUENT: I've used one of my paintings as cover art, my Lunch Break painting for my Lunch Break collection of short stories and poems, but given the wonderful artists we represent in the gallery, it's great to be able to make good use of their extraordinary talents too, whenever possible.

I'm honored to have one of our gallery's most successful and popular painters, Bryan Larsen, creating a series of five paintings as cover art for the *Idolatry* series.

The images, of a woman's hand touching and caressing various parts of a male nude sculpture carved in marble, very much capture the sensuality and passion at the heart of the story, the cherishing and celebration of the human form — the human body, soul, and mind.

SADYE: Where do you find your inspiration?

QUENT: Everywhere. While the religion and philosophy influence more significant, longer work, inspiration for my short stories, plays, flash fiction, and poetry can come from a brief interaction with an elderly woman in the grocery store, from a news article about immigration, from a moment in the park with friends, from a few lines of conversation overheard between strangers in a bar.

(Admittedly, I eavesdrop when working in public places.) People and their stories, in all their incredible variety and range, never cease to interest and captivate me.

SADYE: Fussy is staffed solely by pet lovers, with six cats and two dogs between the two employees, so we have to ask: Do your pets contribute anything to the creative process?

QUENT CORDAIR

QUENT: Our pup, a border collie and kelpie cross, helps get me out of the house and into the great outdoors for an hour or so daily, healthy for both a writer's mind and body.

One of our cats is very good about reminding me that there is life beyond the desk — as she swipes her tail across my keyboard or between my face and the screen.

Our other feline will remind me, quite verbally, with no provocation and less justification, that I should never lose track of the bottom line such that we might no longer be able to afford food for her (as if!).

But the pets do help keep me grounded, attached to the real world. Their mannerisms and antics will work their way into my stories, too.

There are two dogs in *Idolatry*, both of which play important roles, and a treasured cat, the care for which his owner can't bring herself to leave to chance, which helps save her from not caring whether she lives or dies in the pursuit of her dangerous profession.

SADYE: Besides being a short-story writer, you've written novels that mirror your love of romantic art. How much of yourself do you project into your work?

QUENT: I think of it less as projecting myself into my work than as the work being a projection of me.

The art is an extension of my values, a creation out of my own interests, of my own interests, reflecting my personal concerns and wants, my most treasured desires and passions.

Because I create for the pleasure of experiencing what I've created, I create what I hope to most enjoy — if I can manage to pull off the creation of it successfully.

Making art can be one of the most wonderfully selfish, most deeply and intimately rewarding activities in which a person can engage, with the closest equivalent, I think, being making love.

SADYE: What has been your proudest or most satisfying writing moment?

My Kingdom

QUENT: It may have been while I was listening for the first time to the audio files sent by my narrator for his reading of the audiobook edition of *Genesis*, the first part of *Idolatry*.

That was a year or two after I had written and published the ebook and paperback editions, and being able to hear the lines fresh for the first time in a while.

And that was truly special, being able to hear the words come, word after word, and through the most meaningful passages the words being right, so right that I wouldn't think of changing one of them.

Having the words add up to a meaning so intensely and personally meaningful to me — it brought tears.

Writing can be such difficult, challenging work — sometimes it's grueling, sometimes it's terribly frustrating — but there's nothing I can imagine enjoying more, when I can get the writing right.

—Sadye Scott-Hainchek

Published June 22, 2018
The Fussy Librarian
@ www.thefussylibrarian.com

"The Fussy Librarian is the first website to match readers not only with the genre of books they like but also their preferences about content."

If you've enjoyed this work, a short review on Amazon or Goodreads would be greatly appreciated. Thank you truly for your support and assistance.

*   *   *

To alert the author to any errors or typos in the text or to offer any comments, please email **dobby@cordair.com**
or contact the author via **Facebook**.

For the latest Cordair fiction and news, please visit the author's website at
www.quentcordair.com
or
visit the author's Amazon page.

Thank you!

Also by Quent Cordair

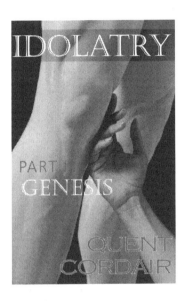

Idolatry Part I: Genesis

In the twilight of the Roman Empire, a sculptor struggles to keep an 800-year dream alive while honoring the love of his life and raising his adopted son. Part I of the epic five-part Idolatry series, the story of a wealthy young heir and a devout Christian girl who find themselves at the heart of a 2400-year struggle for the soul of Western Civilization.

> *"Beautifully written, on the order of Ken Follett's Pillars of the Earth, with the historical insight of James Michener, it brings to life a time of great thought, great art, and its clash with religious fanaticism. Cordair writes with a poet's sense of scene and nuance and gives us a great deal of insight into the mind of a sculptor."* ~ Alan Nitikman

**Available through Amazon
in Kindle, paperback, & audiobook editions**

Idolatry Part II: A New Eden

Journalist Paige Keller, while recovering at a remote resort from an overseas assignment, is drawn into a community dominated by a fundamentalist church, a family of real estate developers, and a group of environmentalists, all in conflict over control of the valley's future. She goes undercover to discover what lies beneath the church's rituals and sacred ceremonies, but the more she learns, the deeper the valley's mysteries and seductions become.

A NEW EDEN is the second part of the acclaimed IDOLATRY saga, the story of a wealthy young heir and a devout Christian girl who find themselves at the heart of an age-old struggle for the soul of Western Civilization.

**Available through Amazon
in Kindle, paperback, & audiobook editions**

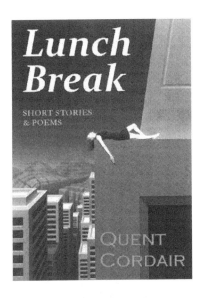

The *Lunch Break* Collection

In *Lunch Break*, a collection of short stories and poems by Quent Cordair, adventure, suspense and romance rule the day as the protagonists pursue their ends with passion and perseverance. The collection includes stories originally published in *The Atlantean Press Review* and *ART Ideas*.

Available through Amazon
in Kindle & paperback editions

Quent Cordair Fine Art
The Finest Romantic Realism
In Painting & Sculpture
www.cordair.com

The fiction of Quent Cordair
resides at ~

"As It Should Be"
quentcordair.com

Made in the USA
Middletown, DE
03 June 2022